DEHISCENT

ASHLEY DENG

Cover Art & Illustrations by Ivy Teas

Edited by Alex Woodroe

TENEBROUS

10p

PRESS

Published by Tenebrous Press.
Visit our website at www.tenebrouspress.com.

First Printing, August 2023.

Print ISBN: 978-1-959790-90-7
eBook ISBN: 978-1-959790-91-4

Cover art & interior illustrations by Ivy Teas.

Jacket design by Alex Woodroe & Matt Blairstone.

Edited by Alex Woodroe.

Formatting by Lori Michelle.

ALSO FROM TENEBROUS PRESS:

To my 公公 and 婆婆, my 爺爺 and 嫲嫲, whose gardens and homes have been a constant companion throughout my life.

DEHISCENT

1 In botany, dehiscence occurs when a plant, at maturity, splits across its structural lines of weakness and releases its contents for distribution, consumption, or regrowth.
2 In anatomy, it is a wound, reopened, split along its lines of healing.

THE OLD ZHU family house sat on stilts high along a cliffside overlooking the East China Sea. It became increasingly familiar with the ocean waves as the years passed, the tides rushing in and up, crashing against straining wood and jagged rocks as they receded, the water levels creeping higher and higher up its stilts, stretching to greet it with each kiss of seaspray.

No one quite knew how long it had been standing— certainly long enough to have seen a time before the summers lasted nine months of the year, when the ocean was calm and clear, distantly below it. It was old enough to have watched the rise of cities full of steel and glass, watching them vacate and implode like a stately, dignified elder.

Yi had lived in this house for all twelve years of her life. She shared the bedroom that once belonged to her father and grandfather when they, too, were children, surrounded by the same furniture and osmanthus branches, the same wooden walls and their bunches of chrysanthemum. Its windows looked out toward what was left of the outskirts of a city once known as Shanghai, the world beyond her windows dusty, barren, and oppressively humid. Her room was farthest from the violent fathoms of the ocean below, but she could still feel the creaking of the house as the winds and waters pulled on its supports; the way the bricks and tiles slid across each other, the way the wood panels held onto each other like bones.

She didn't know much about her family's home because, well, what did it matter to her, really? The house was everything: it protected them from the two months of blistering cold when winter finally arrived, the chill and frost seemingly never penetrating its walls; and when the weather swung hard and the nearby village's food supply suffered and died from the heat, her family always had food, always managed to find what they needed in the nooks and crannies of their house. Because the Zhu house provided, as it always had and as it always will.

One thing she did know was that it always felt a little confused, not that she had the words to describe why. It was a hobbled mix of nineteenth century European and traditional Chinese, with roof tiles of oak and bamboo and terracotta. Outside, it was covered in a healthy dose of grime and dust, the ocean winds kicking up decaying flora that settled into the tiles and brick, gluing them down with salty mist. On the inside was an array of ceramic pots, filled with an equally varied collection of ferments and pickles, from jiuniang to bakfuru to huagua; there were glass jars that held old animal specimens from a long-dead ancestor who was fond of dead things; snippets of aged paper with family recipes, some scrawled by hand and others printed on neat white paper in crisp black letters. Throughout the house was a scattered timeline of increasingly obsolete technology, interspersed by leafy choy that sprouted from the shelves and the ever-replenishing cupboards of canned fish and bottles of sauces.

This was home—an enduring protector of the Zhu family from the outside world—and Yi knew every inch of it.

At least, she knew every inch except the attic.

Once, when she was eight and filled with more energy than she could dispose of, the world was set aflame. It felt as though a blazing inferno had scraped through the atmosphere between the hazy clouds and the dry, dead land below. The Zhu house, while sufficiently adept at keeping out the cold, had always struggled with the heat. It would seep through the walls as the temperatures rose, flooding the house with tepid, humid air, and Yi, like any other child whose pent-up energy was smothered by the elements, went looking for an escape.

Her first idea was to roll under her bed next to the mung bean sprouts and her jarred collection of bones, hoping that the shade would help—though afterward she questioned the impulse in the first place; it was a stupid idea because when was the shade ever actually cooler? It wasn't long before the heat, combined with the semi-enclosed space, turned suffocating, like all the hot air in her room was being siphoned into the space between the floor and her bed. She crawled back out and laid on the floor facing the ceiling as she tried to breathe. Above her, the vines of the mountain yam swayed with the gentle draft that slipped through the windows. Yi got to her feet and trudged downstairs. It wasn't any cooler out there.

Her parents and grandparents sat around their mahjong table in the company of an old historical drama playing on the screen of a staticky CRT. They were in the middle of a game when Yi stomped downstairs and wailed something to the effect of "HOT!"

Attention dropped from their game. Her grandmother nudged her father, a quick but gentle backhanded slap on his arm. "Go look after your daughter," she said.

Yi pouted, crossing her arms. "*Hot*," she repeated.

Her mother slipped out of her chair and knelt on the ground to look at Yi face on. She was sweating too, her face flushed red, strands of hair stuck to her forehead. She frowned sympathetically, then glanced at Yi's father who, after a brief moment, gave a curt nod. "How about a cold shower?" she suggested.

Yi nodded, desperately clinging to the impossibility behind the word "cold"—but her parents suggested it, and that usually meant they knew something she didn't. Still, she said, "But the shower's always hot."

"Upstairs is colder," her mom reassured her. "Promise." She got to her feet and took Yi's hand. "Let's go—I'll help you."

Cold water was an anomaly in the Zhu house. Not that the water was *always* as warm as the sun; sometimes it even ran slightly colder than lukewarm. But cold—true cold—was rare unless they had been recently hit by a blustering polar vortex, and when that happened, well, no one wanted cold water.

The Zhu house still tried to care for them. It gave them soap and clear water, and it maintained a brightness of water lilies and lotuses to balance against the musk of the wood ears and shitakes and king oysters. The bathroom was a pocket of flora that thrived in the dampness that was beyond even what the atmosphere's constant humidity provided. Their tiles were wet and their mats were moss-laden, an ecosystem in and of itself, the last of its kind.

Yi's mother ran the shower and water sputtered out in bursts before it finally calmed to a steady stream pouring out the shower head. The air around them brightened as it cooled down, the water wicking away the murky humidity in favour of new droplets, little pricks of starlight on Yi's face. Her mother helped her strip down and Yi stepped in, feeling the heat melt off her and letting the sweat wash out of her hair. She felt clean for the first time in months, no thin layer of sweat on her skin, no pollution gunk sitting in her pores. She didn't want to leave. In that moment it didn't matter that her

mother leaned in and almost drowned herself, letting the water wet her face and slide over her nose and mouth, the water slowly flooding eyes and orifices, an overflow of relief replacing the quiet suffering in the heat. But Yi, small and preoccupied, just took in the cold, and then panicked when her mother jerked backward, coughing out water as she sat with her arms over the bathtub's sides.

"I'm okay," said her mom between coughs. She waved off Yi and turned away. "Stay here, I'll be back." She tapped the tub once before heading off.

Yi knew she should be troubled, concerned, but she didn't know just *how* much concern she should have. Her mom was going to be okay, right? Her mom was always going to be okay. Her parents looked after her, they would always look after her. So she stayed in the shower until she was tired of being wet and then shut off the water before her mother returned. She dragged her clothes on, still wet, and remembered her mother's words: *upstairs is colder.* There was another upstairs in this house, wasn't there? Among the goji and jasmine bushes that sprouted haphazardly along its walls, there were more stairs that went up, up, up—

Being wet barely shielded her from the heat; sure, it took longer for it to reach her skin but the humidity still lingered in the air outside the bathroom, quickly filling her lungs. Her feet slapped against the wooden floors, leaving puddles wherever she walked. She passed the spare room with the sewing machine—the once-bedroom had been converted into a workroom, full of scrap materials and the garments that were made out of them—then the pile of bedsheets by the staircase, not yet put away. She stood at the base of the stairs that led to the attic, flicked on the lights, and stared.

She'd never been up there before. The second floor of the house was distinctly different from the rest of it, newer and of a style clearly foreign from what she'd seen elsewhere. The attic was no exception, and its dark wood sucked in any light that made it this far. The plants here didn't care; they sat like guardians, their branches reaching out as if in warning. Elsewhere the plants helped give the house some warmth. Not here. The jasmine scent was almost nauseating. The attic had always been an unspoken forbidden, a place she'd never seen the inside of and never seen any of her family entering or leaving. It was a permanently closed door with a permanently shut-off light. Even just standing there, with the light on, the staircase felt too yellow, too cold, too naked. Her heart beat in her ears. Maybe that coldness was a good thing.

She'd made it halfway up the stairs when her dad came barrelling in. She jumped when she heard him bellow her name, almost falling backward down the stairs. Her dad caught her despite her wet skin and damp clothes—because that's what her parents were for—to protect her even when it was her own mistakes—and carried her down.

"What do you think you were doing?" he asked. He was stern, but not angry.

"Mama said upstairs is colder—"

"Not the attic. Don't go up there, okay? It's dangerous."

"Why?" She was scared now. The combined brush with the unknown and the scolding of a disappointed parent made her head swirl with all the words that could surround *dangerous*. She pictured a room full of knives or knife-sharp teeth, where the last sleeping tiger could be awakened, its claws eager to dig into its prey. She'd only seen tigers in her books and the old TV shows they had, and their big mouths and glistening white teeth scared her the most.

Her dad brought her back downstairs and placed her in an empty spot in the living room. He was damp now too, the impression of her tiny body dark on his clothes where he held her. "It's too full," he replied. "Lots of people have lived here and we had to put their belongings somewhere."

Yi pouted, the image of a sleeping tiger whisked away and replaced with piles of junk. "What if there's cool things in there, though?" she exclaimed, full of thoughts of old books and working tech. What about the other kids? What toys did they leave behind?

Her grandmother—slim, gaunt, but unbreakable—interjected before her dad could respond, pointing to them from the dining table where she sat. "*Aiyaa* . . . Look at her. She's going to get sick. Amuy, come here. Sit. Baba will get you a towel." She poured Yi a cup of steaming water as Yi reluctantly took her seat at the table.

"I want cold water, Amah," Yi muttered, frowning. "It's too hot." She watched her dad disappear back up the stairs. She was slowly heating up again and the thought of drinking hot water nauseated her.

"Drink," insisted her grandmother. "It's better for your health."

Frowning deeper, Yi raised the cup to her mouth and took a sip.

On the days that weren't too hot or too cold, Yi went into the village for school. She was the only kid in her class (the only kid at the *school*, she noted sometimes) who lived outside the village, and she was a little jealous that no one else had to walk as far as she did. In part because she really didn't like the walk past—and sometimes through—the old buildings, and in part because even on the most tolerable of days, it was hot, sticky, and hard for her to breathe. Her mom packed her bag with her books and lunch, and handed her a parasol to shield her from the sun. Not that it ever helped much. The trip always made her sweaty and the humidity stuck to her bones and coated her skin and sometimes she wondered if the air in her lungs was as grey as the air that hung between the clouds and the dirt. Apparently, this type of air was called *smog*, according to her teachers, but she didn't understand the point of making the distinction in the first place. It wasn't like the air was ever anything else.

It was as moderate as the temperature ever got; thick,

sludgy, and just balmy enough that the sun wasn't boring into her head. If asked, her parents would probably call it pleasant, but she always thought that description sucked. "Pleasant" to Yi meant comfort, happiness, like the days when she was stuck inside during an ice storm and the indoors temperature—still warm and toasty—was a welcome embrace from the cold outside. "Pleasant" was helping her grandmother wrap dumplings and zongzi in the afternoon as an excuse to escape homework. For Yi, it was hard to call the weather pleasant when it was perpetually grey and heavy, a fine dampness lacing the air. She still accepted that it was better than the alternatives.

The road into the village was littered with houses, growing denser as she neared. In a way, they mirrored the Zhu house, if individually, as there were some in the old, traditional style, and others were the crumbling ruins of what were once modern apartments, the dying bodies of tall and foreboding beasts and their many empty eyes. She didn't like those ones. They were cold, empty, and unnaturally uniform. The decay and the ruins, she thought, made them both better and worse.

The village of Fengxian hadn't always been a village. It was, in fact, once part of the urban sprawl, and the remnants of the fallen suburb were laid out around it, the cluster of houses and apartments, the network of streets and former railroads. But this was where the people congregated after the city and its infrastructure fell, those who had ignored the signs of the collapsing governments and failed security systems. Families fled in clusters to protect each other, huddling in the skeletons of apartments and duplex houses, clinging to the occasional flicker of power feeding in from the cabling established so many decades ago and repaired with patchworked wires. Others got out earlier, found refuge elsewhere in the country, but their fate was the same: crops weren't built for such extremes and livestock couldn't survive, so build your community, keep each other together, keep each other fed. Fengxian was just one of many communities built from the shambles of society, re-learning how to live without modern infrastructure and discovering how to survive the desolation. It probably wasn't even the real name of the area, not that anyone cared anyway.

Yi arrived just as the other kids were starting to settle in for the day. School was usually held in the courtyard when the sun wasn't too strong and the winds weren't ripping through the sand between the buildings. They grabbed mats made of scavenged carpet and tarps and sat in the shade of the apartments surrounding the village; just a slightly grubby group of kids a few years apart, restless to have the day be over before it even began. Yi took a tarp from the pile, thick and sturdy, and wiped off the dust sitting on top of it. Her hand came away plastered in grey-brown. She frowned, fairly sure these had been used recently, as she scraped off the dust from her hand with the side of the tarp. The plastic edge scratched her palm but she figured it was better than smearing it on her clothes.

"No AC today," came a voice from behind her. It was one of her classmates, Qianfan, whose face hadn't quite lost his baby fat just yet. He shook his head and pulled off a carpet from the pile. Yi was fairly sure he was a year younger than she was, but she'd never asked. She didn't like to talk too long with the other kids. The chances of them asking her questions was too high. "Being outside sucks," continued Qianfan, pouting.

"Being outside means we don't have to do writing, though," replied Yi. School was held inside when the power was actually working, in one of the old complexes that had desks, chairs, and writing boards. They were too cumbersome to carry outdoors in the morning and drag back inside at the end of the day, so writing lessons were spare and dependent on factors completely out of anyone's control. In a way, it helped the kids learn at more or less the same pace, despite the age differences. That was important, not just to the adults of Fengxian but to those running the facilities. They wanted the kids to be prepared enough to take over the systems they'd cobbled together once they were old enough to, and while the schools of technology and engineering had fallen along with the rest of society, they were still going to make an effort. Mostly, Yi just understood that she hated the memorization of vocabulary and cramming in as many lines as she could in each of the boxes on her rough-textured papers, especially since her parents still made her practise at home.

Qianfan nodded in agreement, with his big eyes and his round face soft and pleased with this answer. "Yeah, you're right," he said. "Writing sucks more."

As the kids took their seats on the ground, Yi spotted their teacher, Xie Laoshi, at the end of the edge of the courtyard. Normally, she was already standing in front of the kids, ready to lay out the day for the class. But this time, she was in the opening of the alleyway between the buildings that Yi came through, wearing a grey fabric mask over her face as the wind barrelled past her. Yi leaned back to see; Xie Laoshi was only ever over in that area to greet the suppliers—the deliverymen who trucked in on old, sputtering vehicles with a small supply of rations from the complex up north, going around the villages to trade food and water in exchange for the ready-mades the villagers had prepared. Like the clothes Yi's family scavenged together and distributed to the village. Usually they came at the beginning of the week. Usually at the beginning of the day. Yi wasn't here often enough to know the details of their schedules.

Xie Laoshi waved them in. She was a slender woman, though not very tall, and always kept her hair shaved close to her head. Her jacket—made of a thin fabric, just past her torso and pinned where the collars crossed around her waist—whipped around her. She stepped aside as the suppliers entered the courtyard and the fabric fell, calm now that it was free from the wind.

The truck crawled into the courtyard; two men sat in the cabin and one in the open door, hanging on by the frame. Its back was open but covered with a black tarp, tied down over the boxes of cargo. They were still well away from where the kids were seated, but Yi could smell the exhaust, bitter and acrid. It was an old vehicle, probably barely used even before the collapse, and it was a miracle it was working at all. But the trucks and cars used right before everything fell apart were electric, and electricity was just as sparse as gas and harder to reliably put to use. The truck came to a halt with a puff of black smoke.

"Should try to get the others going," said Xie Laoshi, stepping away from the exhaust cloud. "This—" she gestured at the smoke "—this is why we're in this mess."

"Da Ying is trying," said the first of the suppliers as he slammed shut the truck door. "They aren't exactly making it easy for us up there. Energy for the crops is more important than the trucks but they say they're working on it. Something about repairing panels. Until then, we deal with the stench." He walked around the back of the truck and he, along with the other two suppliers, worked to unhook the tarps from the truck bed.

The facility was a mystery to Yi, from their growing and scavenging methods to their distribution; they wore uniforms, a dark, muddied green with worn seams and faded patches that implied some kind of organization but still fit in with the improvised nature of the rest of Fengxian: old, scavenged, and scrambling to make sense. But whoever ran the facility—or facilities, she didn't know—was trying to help, distributing food and whatever else they found that the villagers might need. And watching the way the people of Fengxian funnelled out of their homes, discussing who should take what and how much of each, queueing next to the truck once agreements were made, Yi thought of her house and its food and how she'd never had to ration anything in her life.

DEHISCENT

The suppliers handed out packages wrapped in old newspaper and dirty plastic bags and it occurred to Yi just how thin everyone was, how she should maybe smuggle food out of the house and pass it around. That was what the suppliers did, wasn't it? No one questioned where the food came from and they never asked for anything in exchange— the house could fulfill that duty, it already was. It'd probably be better than handfuls of rice and cured sausage, or whatever else the suppliers brought. Scraps, barely nutritional.

There was a brief moment of activity in the courtyard as the villagers took their packages and dispersed, the chatter among them inaudible beneath the howling wind. The suppliers threw the tarp back over the truck bed and a brisk, cold breeze sliced through the air.

Xie Laoshi took her spot in front of the class, frowning. "That's not a good sign," she said, tucking her jacket into her belt. "Or maybe it's a good sign if you don't want to be in school."

Yi couldn't stop staring at the truck. It struggled on its way out of Fengxian, a cloud of black smoke trailing behind it, thick and swelling until it burst into the grey-orange of the atmosphere above. She watched it shrink into the distance between taking a turn north and abruptly stopping in its place. Xie Laoshi was already laying out the lesson plan for today, interjecting briefly with a comment that class might be cut short due to the encroaching cold, but Yi wasn't really listening. She hated when school ended early, it made her commute feel like a waste. But she was also too transfixed on the suppliers, scrambling out of their truck to get behind it to push. They looked like figures she'd see on her TV, far away and barely real.

Winter came with an urgency, a polar vortex crashing downwards from the arctic circle. The old mercury thermometer they hung by the front door dropped forty degrees in twenty-four hours and Yi watched it patiently, waiting for the mercury to settle at the bottom so she wouldn't have to travel into the village for school. Xie Laoshi had been right to cancel school early the other day; the sudden cold front practically chased Yi home once they were dismissed. It wasn't that she hated school, it was nice to be with her peers, her friends, even, if she dared to call them that. But she dreaded going back so early when she could be at home with her things—her TV, her cards, her family. She was relieved when her parents suggested she wait another day, despite the mercury rising again, millimetre by millimetre, degree by degree.

Yi sat at her desk, bored and avoiding homework. She let her gaze wander the walls and shelves of her living room, past the creaky altar nestled in the corner with its dusty fabric flowers, incense, fruit, and pale figurines watching over her as she did her work; Guan Yu and Guan Yin stared blankly at her, as though war and mercy took their turns scolding a child over her math lessons. There was a couch, worn and sagging, beneath a wall of faded portraits, calligraphy, and photographs depicting the city in its hey-day. A bright pack of soy jutted out of the wall inside of a picture frame, in various stages of growth, from sprout to pod. Next to her desk was a cabinet, its doors made of glass and showcasing decades- if not centuries-old antiques; an array of porcelain lacquer plates, teapots, and bowls, arranged amongst the glass specimen jars that took up any empty space not occupied by the branches of gingko that occasionally cluttered the cabinet with fallen leaves and stinking, acrid fruit.

Gingerly, Yi closed her books. The clutter didn't particularly bother her, but the house was a disorganized mess and frankly, cleaning it up was more interesting to her than homework. She doubted her parents would complain. The CRT buzzed away in the background as she stood in the middle of the living room and contemplated where to begin.

DEHISCENT

After a moment, she picked a corner—across from the altar, where the bright, leafy choy along the walls strained for the residual sunlight from the dusty windows—and got to work.

She gathered all the books in the room, carrying them in her arms and stacking them in a pile in front of the TV. Behind them was another animal specimen, a little white skeleton in an equally small jar whose label was dry and flaking, which she pocketed for her collection upstairs. Next were the papers, dozens of them, from snippets of newspaper and magazines to recipes that she was fairly sure none of her family ever referenced in the first place. She pulled down a roll of newspaper that was stuck on the wall, revealing a blank spot behind it. That was where the old patch of strawberries grew, she remembered. But she had eaten so many that she'd gotten sick of them and now strawberries only seemed to appear occasionally inside the house. And not in this spot, either. The new strawberries grew in the kitchen cabinet behind the mugs.

She glanced at the newspaper in her hand. It was dated 2005. She was surprised it wasn't crumbling in her hands already. She tossed it over to the pile of books and it fell apart then, breaking into shards and dust. Sighing, Yi walked into the kitchen, past her mother and grandmother who were sorting through a table covered in scrap fabric to be sewn into garments. She opened the tiny closet at the far end of the house, where they kept the cleaning supplies, unhooked the duster, and gently clicked the door shut.

"Yi, what are you doing?" asked her mother.

"Cleaning," Yi replied. She was supposed to be doing homework, but she hoped this was a good enough deflection.

"Good luck," said her mother, a small smile tugging at her lips. Her grandmother opened her mouth to say something, but her mom shook her head. "No, no, let her figure it out."

"Figure what out?" asked Yi. She frowned, eyeing her mom.

"You'll see," her grandmother replied, nodding. "When you're done, Amuy, I'll make you some baktonggoh."

"Mama—"

"Listen to Amah," her mother insisted. Her tone was playful yet bored, as though she had expected Yi to know what they were talking about by now and was amused that she hadn't figured it out yet.

Yi looked down at the duster in her hand and swung it a little, half expecting something to happen then and there—that it might transform into a snake, that the individual feathers would start to twirl and writhe, that they might separate and bare sharp, white teeth. Nothing happened. It was just a piece of plastic with brown feathers sticking out of it and nothing more. She glanced back at her mom and grandmother before returning to the living room, whatever pride she had in taking up the task quickly turning to unease.

In the living room, her work stared back at her. The papers, the books, the pictures, and the jars—they were displaced, sitting uncomfortably in their new locations. The spaces they left bare and beckoning for their missing occupants. Yi frowned. When had this house last been cleaned? Did anyone even try? *Whatever*, she thought, shrugging. This shouldn't take long. A quick dusting would do the trick. Starting from the corner, she held her breath and swept the dust that had lovingly embraced the wood of the house. It bloomed in clouds around her, and as her lungs started to scream for air, Yi waved away the dust, feeling it stick closely to her skin and settle into her pores. She was going to need a shower after this, just like after coming in from outside; the grime and dust pulling away the feeling of being clean. Clean the house and get dirty in the process, apparently.

Yi did what she could. The top shelves were harder for her to reach and she wasn't able to push aside the cabinets to clean behind them, so there was a thin layer of dust that started at the ceiling and ended just above Yi's reach, with the uppermost pictures untouched and the plants jutting out of the walls and shelves swaying slightly after their brief brush with the feather duster. She didn't touch the altar. That felt more like her parents' jurisdiction. Instead, she turned her attention to the cabinet next to her desk where the empty eyes of a jarred snake skin waited for her care.

The cabinet doors were dusty like everything else in the house, giving the glass the look of having been glazed over or frosted. She used the knuckle of her pinky to draw a line in the filth, and the dust piled up at the end of the trail; clean glass like a river among trees. Using a page from a newspaper, she wiped her finger clean and got back to work. First were the doors, then . . .

She looked through the glass, to the jars of dead animals floating in brown liquid that no one ever touched, then to the other jars, of fermenting rice and cabbage and mustard greens and citrus fruits. Those ones—*those* her family touched, and the little, slightly less dusty circles beneath them gave that away. The gingko branches nestled in tightly with the jars and photographs were bright yellow, their pale orange fruit soft and squishy and covered in a thin layer of powdery white. They looked mature, just about to drop. Mature enough that Yi knew it would stink once she opened the cabinet. She took the two circular handles in her fingers, held her breath, and opened.

With the new rush of air, so too came the smell of rot. Yi stumbled backward, still coughing at the sudden stench of rotting excrement. The fruit were so appetizing otherwise— they looked like they should be sweet, peach-like even, and every time, always caught her by surprise. She fell into her chair and sat searching for fresh air.

Yi closed the cabinet and adjusted her seat, the legs of her chair rumbling against the floor like the sound of blood rushing in her ears. She froze. That was louder than it should have been.

Slowly, she turned around.

The books, the papers, the photographs and their frames, they were all back where she had found them, no longer in piles waiting to be sorted and organized anew. Everything had found their homes again, but at least the dust was all gone.

Yi's mom walked past the living room door, her arms full with scrap fabric to be cleaned out in the foyer at the other side of the house. She smiled at Yi. "Well? How did it go?" she asked, her tone as playful as before.

Yi didn't know what to say. She reached for her pen and rolled it in her fingers. Maybe she should've just stuck to homework after all. "Bad," she replied, finally. "I think. Does it . . . does it always do that?"

Her mom shrugged apologetically. "This place is hard to keep clean," she said. "I tried once, when I first met your father. What can I say? I don't think it wants to be cleaned up."

Yi wanted to ask *How?* How could everything she moved, everything she touched, be re-shelved and re-hung as though nothing had happened at all? But she looked to the mushrooms growing in the cabinet just next to her shoulder, then to the patch of soy on the wall, and swallowed down the question.

The front door opened as Yi was attempting to get back to her homework. It was her father, dirty and sweaty, back with scraps from the town ruins. He tossed the duffel bag into the hallway and it slumped as it landed, the zipper hitting the floor. More fabric scraps to sort through, clean, and sew into garments.

Her parents exchanged a few words, too quietly for Yi to hear, before her mother left for the foyer. Yi looked up from her work, her dad popping his head into the living room and her mom running the tap to fill the plastic basin for washing. "Mama said you tried to clean the house?"

"Just this room," Yi muttered. She felt embarrassed, as though she was caught doing something so obviously impossible she should never have thought to do it in the first place. She wanted to change the subject to anything but her stupid mistake. She'd even accept questions about her homework. Maybe something interesting she learned recently. She glanced at her dad. "Is it really bad out?" she asked.

He shook his head. "Humid," he said. "But we've had worse." He leaned over to slide the duffel bag further into the house, toward the kitchen. "You'll probably be going to school again soon. Maybe tomorrow even. I'm sure your friends haven't stopped all this time."

"Yeah . . . " She glanced at her homework again. Were they even her friends? She barely made the attempt. "How—How about the day after? So I can uh, really make sure all my work is done."

"If you do it now, you can really make sure all your work is done," he replied with a grin. "Instead of trying to clean the house."

"I thought it would be productive."

Her dad leaned on the door frame, arms crossed over his chest. The wind whistled past and rattled the house and Yi could hear the waves crashing below her through the fizzy static of the CRT. "How much homework do you have?"

Yi stammered, searching for an answer. She knew—they both knew—that the homework her teacher assigned was more of a thing to keep the kids busy, to encourage their growth and to cover basic skills, sure, but it was ultimately without any real consequence, given the amount of kids in different age groups in the same class. Still, she should be doing it, even with the world in the state it's in. They should all be learning, as Xie Laoshi said.

"You know what," said her dad. "Let's go show you how to fix up the house."

"What?" asked Yi. She gestured at the walls, then the floors, then jabbed a thumb at the pile of gingko fruit in the cabinet next to her. "Since when did it need fixing?"

Her dad just smiled. "Come on! I'll show you."

Yi's dad brought them outside, but she really didn't want to. He was right; it was humid but not yet sweltering, caught somewhere between the chill of the polar vortex and the inherent heat of the atmosphere, and frankly, it sucked. She hated sweating when the breeze felt cold. They stood at the edge of the cliff, tools in hand, looking out over the water and the algae-covered wood panels of the house. Her dad held up his metal scraper to show her how to hold it, and started at the side of the house. The algae sludged off, thick and slimy.

"I thought we were fixing things," said Yi. She looked down at her own scraper, wide and plastic with a tiny nub for a handle. She wasn't sure this was better than homework. Maybe her dad was punishing her. "This isn't fixing."

"The house provides," said her dad. "But that doesn't mean it doesn't need maintenance. We have to take care of it and it'll take care of us." He ran his scraper along a long panel, the algae building up on the blade in a pile of murky green. In one swift motion, he flung the algae into the water; the sound of its splash was drowned out by the waves.

Yi tried to get a look, leaning over the precarious edge. She could see the stilts as they met the water and where the house met the cliff. Everything was brown. Even the waters roiled with a murkiness that held billions of tiny particles, the plastic shards, the beads of long-dead, calcified animalia, all suffocating the breath of the ocean. "Cleaning off gunk? To preserve the wood?"

"Yep," her dad replied. He gestured at the algae. "Think about it—all of this will eat away at the house and we don't want that."

"Sure," Yi muttered. She lifted her scraper and followed her dad, getting as close to the edge as she dared, then cautiously returning the algae to the sea. She wondered if that helped the ocean at all, if some of that greenery, as gross as it was, was better off in the waters below. She caught a glance at the ocean-facing side of the house and said, "What about back there?"

"Ah, that's tricky," said her dad, rubbing his eyes. "It involves climbing upstairs and using ropes and—"

"Like the attic?"

"Sure. I'll show you one day. We'll do the pipes first. And the door hinges. The lights, too. You should learn about the wires."

"Baba, come on," continued Yi. "What's in the attic?"

He paused mid-stroke. Quiet and deep in thought, he finished scraping his line of algae and threw it away. "Don't go in there," he said finally. "You have a lot to learn about this house before you can tackle that one, okay? It's just full of junk and I don't want you getting hurt." He tapped her shoulder reassuringly and started again. "After this, I'll show you where the lightbulbs show up."

It was still cold the day Yi went back to school. Not quite as unbearable as the polar vortex but cold enough that she had to break out the few pieces of warm clothing that she owned. She wrapped herself in a long-sleeved shirt and a jacket that was buttoned up to the neck and straining to keep warmth in. Her parents suspected it was actually going to get cold *again*—some separate cold front that followed the brief reprieve from the polar vortex—but Yi was restless at home, alone and stuck in the house, so they insisted on sending her off. School would be good for her.

That morning, Yi was in the kitchen, packing her bag by herself while her parents were busy setting up the mahjong table in the dining room. It was just her and her grandmother, who scooped out another bowl of congee for Yi, the pidan floating like blackened stones in snow. Yi didn't really want it—she was already warm and the congee was hot enough to make her flushed—but she took it anyway, knowing the guilt she'd feel if she didn't take what was available.

As she ate, she eyed the bundle of longan sitting on the counter, next to the pile of youtiao and pork and mushroom bao fresh out of the steamer. They had so much, more than enough for her family, surely. Maybe she could smuggle some out, split them with the other kids at school, pass them around like they pass around laisee, except this time, these were full, delicious, so much more than a symbolic gesture handed down through the generations to give the kids something to look forward to amidst the desolation.

But, she couldn't do that, could she? The kids would ask— Your family never comes to get rations, they're never with the other grown-ups whose bellies stayed empty so they could feed their kids—where did she get all this food? At best, they'd stare. At worst, they'd accuse. No, they'd probably do more than that. Would Xie Laoshi protect her? Or would her teacher watch as she was torn apart for flaunting her abundance like it was charity?

Yi scarfed down her congee, and with it the image of hands, so many hands, grabbing and pulled and clawing. She'd probably try anyway. It felt so wrong to keep everything to themselves.

She placed the empty bowl in the sink, her grandmother hovering over it as she washed the dishes. Water ran from the faucet and the air smelled like soap—*soap, does anyone else even have soap?* It was such a small, inconsequential thing to be clean but then, Fengxian was barely more than a hastily put-together living arrangement where clean water was a luxury. It showed, too, in the actions of her grandmother. There were slivers of soap piled onto each other in attempts to use up their scraps, bowls full of rice water to water the plants or wash their hair. These were part of life for Yi, but she didn't understand it.

She placed her bag onto the counter, open and mostly empty. It had her papers, a notebook, a few writing instruments, her small, packed lunch. Her fingers were itching to grab and hide, her eyes scanning the counter in front of her; what else could she bring? What else *should* she bring?

She watched her grandmother carefully.

After a moment, Yi slid the bundle of longan into her bag and zipped it closed. She mentally calculated that it probably wouldn't be enough for the twenty-odd kids in her class, and was it even worth giving them a single longan? It seemed like a pitiful snack—but that's all it was, really. A snack, the small luxury of its sweetness, its bright and clean taste. A single longan per kid. She pictured the hungry eyes of her classmates boring into her. No, if she were going to share, she needed to do better.

So, she looked to the pile of bao—fresh, fragrant, and abundant. That might do, but she needed something to bring them to school in. Leaving her bag on the counter, Yi left for the tea room.

Yi often wondered if the tea room was ever used for its intended purpose. Its entrance was a circular opening, camellia leaves and their white flowers budding from the frame. It housed a deep lacquered shelf with teapots, cups, and clay pots and tins filled with loose tea leaves. This was also where they stored their kitchen towels, on the shelf adjacent to the one that held their tea; piles of old, worn towels and napkins, most faded in colour if they hadn't already been white. She only needed a few. Maybe that really big one they had for some reason, the pink one that used to be red with the fraying embroidered edges and was big enough to cover the tea room's table.

She slid her left arm under the pile and pulled the one she wanted out with her right, careful not to disturb the uneven and haphazardly arranged cloths stacked on top of it. Gently, she placed the rest back down. Being careful meant she had to be quiet, and hopefully no one would notice anything missing. Being careful also mean she was slow, and so when she turned around, she was greeted by her grandmother in the doorway.

Yi jumped. "A-Amah," she stuttered. "I, uh, was getting a—"

Her grandmother stepped into the tea room, shaking her head and tutting disappointedly. She placed Yi's bag onto the table, unzipped it, then slowly pulled out the bundle of longan. "You know," she started, placing the longan next to her bag. "You have a good heart—and that's a good thing—but you also need to use your brain, Yi." She tapped her head with a bony finger, thin with age and calloused with use. "This can't go with you."

"It's not fair," said Yi. "You know it isn't. We've got all of these things, Amah. Everyone else—they have scraps."

Yi's grandmother zipped up her bag and handed it to her. She was impassive but grim. "I know," she said. "But you also know why we can't share."

Yi took her bag reluctantly. She stared at the bundle of longan before plucking one off for herself. "No one else knows that the house provides," she muttered as she tore open the paper-like skin. She popped the fruit into her mouth, savouring the floral sweetness, and imagining the reaction from the other kids in the village. They'd be delighted, probably. How often did they get fresh fruit? Or sugar? She tongued the seed away from the flesh, spat the beady black seed into her hand, and licked the sugar from her lips. "Maybe one day?" she offered.

Amah tutted again, holding her hand out. Yi gave her the skin and seed, a pupil taken from its fleshy shell. Her grandmother always took the seeds from their fruits and vegetables and scattered them around the house when no one was looking. Or at least, that's what she thought Amah was doing. She'd never asked. The plants were her grandmother's domain and her domain alone.

"Go on," said Amah, pushing her out into the hallway. "You don't want to be late." She pulled Yi's scarf from the bannister and put it loosely around her neck before heading back toward the kitchen.

DEHISCENT

Yi glanced outside, through the windows that were nestled on either side of the front door. The world looked dead, even more so than usual. Grey and washed out without the warm hues of orange and brown that permeated the atmosphere on most days. She glanced up and could almost see the blue sky in slivers beneath the clouds that sped past, riding the winds high above. She slid on her boots, straightened herself, and took a deep breath.

"Do I have to go?" asked Yi. She eyed the thermometer by the door, the mercury stuck near the bottom where the surrounding mugwort hung its silvery-purple flowers. The cold scared her; it cut into her, pulled the air from her lungs, and never happened frequently enough for her to get used to it.

Her grandmother joined the rest of her family around a game of mahjong, sitting in the middle of the dining room. This was their usual morning game before they got to work sorting through scraps, then cutting and sewing them together. They always started the day with some mahjong and closed it off with mahjong too; their lunchtime games cycled between mahjong and cards, depending on everyone's moods and who was home. The tiles on the felt-topped table glinted a translucent, pale green atop a block of white.

"Dress warmly," replied her mom. "Go see your friends!"

"But come home early!" exclaimed her father over the clangs and clinks of mahjong tiles. "It's going to drop quickly."

Yi glanced at her parents' and grandparents' game before reluctantly wrapping her scarf around her nose and mouth. "What's for dinner?" she asked, hovering at the door. Anything to kill time.

"Ask the house!" said her mother.

Yi stifled a groan, then opened the door.

The air was humid and mild despite the wind, which pierced her like ice and cut her to the bone. The leftover chill of the night hung in crystals around her, melding to her skin as she walked her usual route to the village. There was still frost on the ground, dusting the wispy grass like lace while the sheets of ice crunched underfoot. It was a weird feeling, being cold and humid at the same time; she was sweating under her layers when the surface of her skin still felt so cold.

The abandoned town that led to the village of Fengxian was a looming beast of old infrastructure—the wind played the buildings like instruments, blowing through broken windows and funnelling into open plots kicking up dust and debris in their twisters; they played a song of staccato melodies filled with high, whistling notes that danced in the air. Usually, Yi tried her best to stick to the streets—or at least, whatever was left of them—since they were her most straightforward route to school. But today, as the cold snapped at her face and the wind blew her backward, the walls—or at least, whatever was left of them—shielded her instead of impeded her, and she changed her route to weave through the buildings.

Her bag was disappointingly light, filled instead with the hypothetical that she could share her relative prosperity, to provide a brief moment of joy, of relief, of reprieve. She didn't actually know anything about scarcity, she wouldn't know what it felt like to have nothing and be given everything. But watching the supply distribution, the solemn faces and hungry mouths—she wanted to do something, anything. She was sitting on a pile of goods and comfort and it was terrible knowing all that she had and all that they did not. The house provided, after all.

And no one else could know about it.

Yi, reluctantly, understood. What would people think if they knew the Zhu family had an abundance of whatever they needed? That their food supply was secure, that their home was protected from the elements? What would they do if they learned that they had been hiding resources all this time? She was pretty sure it wouldn't go well. She got it, but she really didn't like it.

DEHISCENT

Yi passed through an empty building that was barely more than crumbling walls, empty door frames, and a partial ceiling. Her usual path was still close by. In fact, she could almost see it through the tunnels of broken walls and door frames. Her steps cracked through the frosty, dead vegetation onto the old concrete. There was a bit of slip underfoot, where the ice was starting to melt but hadn't yet turned to clouds floating in the air, and when she looked down to watch her steps, she noticed mud, tracked in from elsewhere in footprints from a much, much larger shoe than hers. She didn't have a lot of time—school was starting soon—but she wanted to see where the footprints went.

She didn't have to go far. Hunched over in a corner, in the bowels of the old apartment building, there lay a man wearing the uniform of a supplier, knees curled and arms hugging himself for warmth. There wasn't much light coming through here—the ceiling was still up for the most part, if a little dilapidated—but she could make out the details of his face; his eyes closed and his lips blue.

Yi took a step and held her breath, looking for some kind of movement. But the man was still. Hesitantly, she stepped forward again. And again.

This wasn't a good idea and she knew it, but she approached him anyway because what if the man was still alive? What if he needed help? How long had he been there, where were the other suppliers, why had he been left alone?

Yi got a good look at him up close. The man was covered in ice, gradually melting as the world warmed up; there were small droplets that coated his skin and his hair and his clothes, giving him a sheen despite the pallor beneath the humidity. All of his skin had blued in fact; his flesh was now translucent layers of blue and purple, muddied by the layers above. There were small cuts across his skin, uneven pockmarks and streaks that were edged with blood and frost. His clothes were torn, too. Ripped to shreds in places, but still recognizably those of a supplier. Yi searched for signs of his breath, for any small movement of his chest or his lips. And, when she was sure the man in front of her was dead, she knelt down and reached out a shady hand. She couldn't believe she was doing this—touching a dead body—and she didn't even have friends there to egg her on. Because that's what kids did, right? That's what they seemed to do on her shows.

The tips of her fingers broke the frost layer on the corpse's skin, felt the wet fabric. She felt nothing but cold there—he was solid, frozen, and stiff from death.

Yi wanted to vomit; her head spun, light and prickly, as though the wind could pick her up and float her away. She had to tell someone. This body had been here long enough and someone needed to take it away, to identify him and inform his family—but who? Her teacher? She wasn't sure about that. She already worried that Xie Laoshi didn't like her, didn't like that she was coming into the village, was living away from the community. And then scaring the other kids with stories of a dead body? Maybe she was just imagining that part. Maybe it didn't matter at all. Maybe. She didn't want to risk it. Who did that leave, then? The people running the facilities? The elders of Fengxian? How about her parents? Would they let her walk to school on her own if they found out? They could tell the others, probably—adults talking to adults always got more done anyway. She swallowed hard on that decision, still struggling to look away. Her parents it was, then. They'd know what to do.

Yi wiped the moisture from her hands onto her pants and treated back onto her route. She tried to push the image of the corpse to the back of her mind. But his frozen face, his discoloured skin; it didn't help her hate the cold any less.

School had already started by the time Yi got to Fengxian. The clearing was empty when she arrived, and panic prickled up her spine. She was still on edge, as much as she wanted to pretend that everything was okay, to act like nothing happened, holding herself together while the dead supplier floated at the back of her eyes. She touched it—why'd she do that? This wasn't the same as the meat she'd help prepare at home, not like the leather her family scrapped from old furniture. That was a man who had been alive just days or even hours ago, preserved by the wild swing of the climate that killed him. Yi's breath caught in her throat as her panic turned into a chill. She stuffed her hands into her pockets and held herself close, steadying her breath until she could focus on what to do next. She was here for school, except school wasn't *here*.

An old woman waved her down through the window in her home, looking into the clearing. She wore a thin felted vest over a thin sweater, and she was surrounded by bare window dressings that Yi was almost certain must have been her family's handiwork. The woman smiled and pointed her in the direction of the school building—*Inside,* she was saying. *School is inside, today.*

Yi gave the woman a curt bow before running off.

Fengxian tried to keep a few buildings in good condition, mostly the shared living spaces or anything that housed working electronics, and the small, concrete once-library was one of the few that saw any kind of consistent maintenance. The collapse left a lot of things to rot into obscurity and the generations that survived scrambled to maintain what few remnants of a society they'd only heard about through stories. Mostly, people had forgotten what this building once was; now, it housed the sick and the injured, the communicators used to speak with the other villages and compounds, and the kids, when their classes were shuttled indoors. There had been a strong effort made to ensure the building was functional and passably clean. The desks and chairs were old but sturdy, there were stacks of blank, recycled paper, and holes in the ceiling and cracks on the floor where the crumbling tiles and linoleum had been removed.

Yi passed by a handful of adults as she made her way through the halls, each pointing her in the direction of her class. She wanted to tell them that she knew where she was going, that she'd done this trip enough times before, that she wasn't just some helpless, lost kid—but she kept her mouth shut. These were the caretakers of the village. They meant well. She couldn't bring herself to be angry at them for doing their jobs.

The classroom door was wide open when she reached it. Yi felt a tinge of guilt swirling with the rest of her heightened anxiety—did Xie Laoshi leave it open for her? She could see her at the front of the class, writing on the board with small, white stones. Yi almost turned around and left, hating every bit of disapproval she thought she felt pouring out of Xie Laoshi, but she slid into class anyway, slowly, quietly on the balls of her feet. She settled into the first empty seat she could find, and cringed when the chair creaked and the table wobbled and the zipper of her bag was too loud as she pulled out her books. But Xie Laoshi didn't seem to mind. She nodded to acknowledge her presence and continued with the lesson.

Yi relaxed, just a little, now that she knew she wasn't in any trouble, but she could still feel the eyes of the other kids, pecking away at her with short, rapid glances. Yi wished she didn't care. Most of the time, she didn't. Normally, when she caught the other kids staring, she'd glare back at them, challenging them. She hated being the one who everyone singled out, staring at her like an overturned beetle on the windowsill. But today wasn't normal. Today felt like she was standing on the ever-shifting slush of melting ice, just barely thick enough to hold her weight. She wanted to fall through just to get it over and done with.

She'd go home and tell her dad, offload the image that was still floating behind her eyes like the tears she knew were ready to pour. She wanted the comfort of her dad's explanations and plans, the reassurance that this was, in fact, not normal, that life wasn't always going to threaten to fall away with the wind. She didn't want death to be so near to her. She didn't want to think about what happened when people's hearts stopped and their breaths shrank away; not the cold, gummy flesh she felt, not the blank, cloudy eyes. She wanted her dad to tell her that this wasn't a usual occurrence despite the scraps and the rations, despite the world and its cycle of inhabitability.

Yi's hand shook as she took down today's lesson. Partially due to the cold, partially because the vocabulary set contained the word for "person" far too many times.

The wind turned icy by the time class was dismissed. Yi ran home, not just to beat the cold or to avoid the dead supplier in the ruins—she wanted to go home to safety and sanctuary, to the unchanging in an unpredictable, ever-changing world. She raced against the sun, keeping to the sunlit parts of the ruins as rays poked in and out of the clouds, avoiding the nooks behind the rubble and half-standing walls, and she tried hard not to jump at the sight of corpses where there were none. Every little scrap felt like a clue leading her to another body, every pile of rubble covered in tarp was another dead man awaiting her discovery.

She slowed to a cautious walk as she neared the house, breathing hard to catch her breath. And then, as she approached the door, she braced herself. She needed to tell someone about the dead body, she just hoped she wasn't going to scare her family.

Inside, the house was warm and fragrant and quiet; it smelled of soup, brothy and clear, and the earthy palate of wutau kauyuk. Yi shut the door, slipped off her shoes, and removed her bag, leaning it against the bench they kept by the door. There was no sound of mahjong being played, no whir of the sewing machine, no rhythmic cutting or washing or preparing food.

Yi found her grandmother in one of the house's smaller rooms, next to the shelf of fruiting trees, a small pair of scissors in one hand and a skewer and cotton string in the other. She cut off dying leaves and tied sagging stems to sticks, tending to the plants as she always did, despite the house practically breathing with life already. It didn't need the help of anyone else, but that didn't matter. The plants were hers, as though being unable to tend to a garden of her own—one that was outside where the trees could grow to their full heights, where the plants could stretch and commune with the sun—Amah made the plants of the Zhu house her responsibility instead. Yi smiled as she watched her grandmother and listened to the food bubbling away in the kitchen. These were her two ways of showing her love; helping Yi understand the plants and teaching her how to take care of them, and the endless hours she spent carefully crafting Yi's favourite food, often unprompted but always appreciated.

"Go have some soup, Amuy," said her grandmother.

"Of course, Amah," Yi replied. A bowl of soup, warm and slightly bitter and everything that the outside wasn't right now. Maybe it would help the nerves. Maybe it would help her forget, just a little. "Have you seen Baba?"

"He'll be back soon." Her grandmother reached over to a plump yellow mango and plucked it off the bush that was jutting out of the wall. She smiled. "Here, have this too. Your father should be back from his delivery soon."

Yi held the mango to her nose, taking in its sweetness. She forgot today was a delivery day; her father and grandfather were both out to hand off finished garments to the village. She wondered if they saw the body, too.

"Thank you, Amah," said Yi before leaving for the kitchen, taking the mango with her.

DEHISCENT

It was raining by the time her father and grandfather came home. They had gotten lucky, returning just before the drizzle turned into a downpour and the wind battered the house until it shook. Their friend and distribution partner, Guiyu, was less lucky. Even if they wanted to let him in, they really couldn't. Friendships like theirs were perhaps only maintained through secrets.

"Could I come in?" he asked, standing in the doorway while Baba and Ayeh were safe inside. He was gaunt, the shadows playing unfavourably against his deep-set eyes, but he held his arms above his head and the water dripped through his sleeves. It was like a cruel joke of his name to be stuck soaking wet outdoors.

Ayeh hesitated. He glanced at his son wearily before turning to the trunk by the stairs.

"I'm sorry, Guiyu," said Yi's dad. "Our house is a mess. There's nowhere for you to stay."

Yi leaned over in her chair, bowl raised to her lips, straining to see the commotion at the front door. She knew what the outcome was going to be—no one outside of the family is allowed in the house—but she still wanted to know how her father and grandfather were going to land on that conclusion. Lightning struck overhead and the sky lit up a bright white before returning to the cloud ceiling of bright pinks and oranges of a sunset storm. The rain fell in sheets for a minute while Yi's grandfather rummaged among the items in the trunk. Guiyu stepped inside, a single step more than any outsider, as far as Yi was aware.

"Here, here!" said Ayeh, pulling out what he was looking for from the trunk. He held a transparent umbrella, extra material stuffed inside. He shuffled over to Guiyu and opened it; from one end the extra plastic hung loosely around the circumference of the umbrella, but Yi's grandfather handed the umbrella to Guiyu and pulled the plastic around him, zipping it closed around the top. "There!" Ayeh exclaimed. "You'll be safe."

Outside, the rain sputtered and slowed to fat droplets falling lazily from the sky. Guiyu was soaking beneath the umbrella, but he took it reluctantly, eyeing the inside of the Zhu house with wide, suspicious eyes. They settled on Yi and for a brief moment she was reminded of the blank, dead eyes of the supplier frozen in place and starting to pale over.

"You better hurry," said Yi's dad. "Before it starts raining again."

A bright flash of light caught Yi's eye and she looked out the kitchen window to the churning ocean, where the storm rolled on and the lightning continued into the distance.

"I'm already soaked—"

Ayeh started closing the door. "See you next week, Guiyu," he said. "I'll be sure to bring some snacks next time. How about some fish! If we can get any from out there." Another cruel joke of his name.

The front door clicked closed. Ayeh hung his head and patted his son on the arm. He retreated upstairs, probably to change into dry clothes.

Yi dragged her gaze back to her soup. She pretended she hadn't been paying attention to the conversation at the front of the house, her head running. What was she going to tell her dad? Would he even be able to do anything about it? She needed to tell him—he had to know. Or was it more that Yi needed to offload? To bleed and deflate, to do something about the spikes of anxiety growing and sharpening inside her head, until the image bled from her eyes to the rest of the world. She swallowed the last of her soup and regretted it.

"Baba—"

"Yes?" Her father was also quite wet, water still dripping from his hair and the humidity from outside wafted off him in waves of musk and minerals. He wasn't displeased or angry, but he did look tired. He mustered up a small smile.

Yi let it pour: the twisting route she took to class, the suppliers from the other day and the problems they were having with their vehicles, the dead man in uniform found curled up against a decaying wall. She didn't know where to begin or where to end because she kept asking him what they were supposed to do about it, about who was going to look after the body, who would inform his family, about who else she might find on her trips to school. She took in a shaky breath. "Are you going to make me stay home?" she asked. She hadn't realized how much she dreaded that option.

Her dad looked at her, his face solemn and grim. "Don't you worry about it," he said. "We want you to go to school, being here all by yourself isn't healthy."

"But what about—"

"I'll make sure someone takes care of it," said her dad. He squeezed her shoulder and nodded, eyes looking directly into hers. "Try to get a good sleep tonight. Drink your soup, have some tea. Maybe it'll help you forget." He took her bowl and headed to the pot of soup on the stove to refill it.

Yi wanted to forget; that was all she really wanted right now. But she didn't know if she could. That was a dead body and she *touched it* and she knew it was her idea and she knew this was all her fault, but she touched the dead body of a man who was probably just trying to help bring food and water and tea to the village and now he was dead and *she touched it*—Yi took the soup from her father with watery eyes and tried to wash the whole memory away.

The wind rattled the house, slamming into the stone and the wood and shaking something else out of the dark corners between the kitchen shelves; it fell onto the bamboo mat on the floor with a wet *thud*. On the ground next to Yi's chair was a package about the size of her head, wrapped in paper and tied with twine. Sometimes the house dropped things for them rather than sprouting them in the predictable nooks of shelves and drawers; usually of a different nature than the plant stuff or fermented goods. She picked it up, undid the twine, and let the paper unfurl. Inside were various cuts of meat, bright and fresh and laced with white connective tissues and fat. She wasn't sure what kind of meat this was.

It wasn't like she ever saw the animals it came from. The house always provided them with already-butchered cuts of meat, but usually the same kind per package. She slid it to the edge of the table for the grown-ups of the house to deal with.

Meat, flesh, death.

Even the prospect of food circled back to the corpse in the ruins.

That night, her sleep was troubled by hazy glimpses of inexplicable images, accompanied by emotions she didn't know how to classify—overwhelming, nebulous, too much for her brain to process or handle. But her sleep was solid; not even the restless, rumbling storm overhead disturbed her, and she woke in the morning with tears on her pillow from dreams she couldn't remember.

Somewhere, earlier, between the network of facilities that had taken over the once-city of Shanghai and the deadened suburbia-turned-village of Fengxian, there was a man, a problem, and a machine.

This man had a name, he had many names in fact, but they hardly mattered here, especially not when his friends (colleagues, coworkers, what did those words even mean anymore?) preferred to call him by the name of the animal whose traits they claimed he shared: bulging eyes, swollen lips. They still had those fish in the facilities, in purely decorative tanks that bubbled filtered water and shimmered with lotuses. Someone high up liked to keep them for company and the people working there didn't like to test the volatile.

They'd been having sourcing issues, although one could argue they were always having sourcing issues. From nitrogen-rich soil to the chemicals and fibres required to make new filters, the facilities were always running into shortages and the lack of manufacturing ability meant they relied on the people who knew where to find what and how to take them apart, clean them, fix them, make them usable again. Fuel, though. That was harder. Gasoline sat in tanks and went stale, and most of the time the suppliers had to push their trucks back, kilometres at a time, after delivering the rations. The batteries were starting up again, he'd been told. But they needed electricity first.

The man followed a lead handed to him by one of his superiors: over by Fengxian, in the surrounding empty buildings, there had been a server building of some kind, a mass of swirling cables and copper wire that might, hopefully, be of use to the facility.

"Why hadn't we gone there before?" the man asked.

"Who said we hadn't?" came the reply.

"Why didn't they grab it all when they found it?"

"A villager told us. He doesn't want to interfere."

Interfere. That felt awfully close to what he was doing right now.

Before him was a collapsed structure, stinking of rotting wood and covered in debris. It had probably been a house, or a section of a block of buildings that held housing and commerce side-by-side. There were broken machines next to the intact ones sitting on desks. Their screens were coated in dust, their plastic frames chipping at the seams. There were several encased computers that had been strewn onto the floor and cracked open, their internals spilling. And, of course, there were the cables. Many, many cables in faded colours that ran beneath the concrete blocks and into the walls. Behind him, more glass, interspersed with fragments of what looked like toys; the scraps of cute animal smiles sewn onto plastic fabric.

It looked as though the walls had been cleared out recently, with some of the mid-sized concrete blocks moved aside, trails of small debris behind it showing where they'd once sat. These weren't well-explored buildings. They were part of a block or two between the facilities and Fengxian that had been destroyed almost to the point of rubble, and if there were remaining bubbles of prior life, the suppliers had deemed them too dangerous to set foot in. And yet.

Peeking behind a semi-collapsed wall was the server, or at least that's what he was told it was. A wall of machinery, which the wires fed into like a heart.

They should've sent more people, he thought. He couldn't possibly bring this all back on his own.

And then, the wind changed.

It had been warm but not sweltering when he arrived, though the breeze had been picking up ever since he'd stepped out of the facilities. At first it had been cool, but humid. Now, it was sharp; an icy undercurrent that howled through the broken walls. He didn't like that. These winds were too unpredictable.

Debris picked up in a whirlwind, whistling and whipping him with tiny shards of glass and concrete. Covering his face, he stumbled through the collapsed buildings toward something, anything, that'd provide cover.

Was he so disliked by the others? he wondered, pulling his jacket collar as high as he could manage. Was that why he'd been sent alone? To think he might be disposable—this was hardly the time to treat men as such and yet, buffeted by the debris, the fabric tearing from his body, the skin tearing from his flesh, he felt disposable, disposed *of* to be precise. A chill ran through him, whether from the cold or from the blood, and he stumbled through the ruins, collapsing near a broken wall.

The wind burst through the buildings, and it and the pain were loud enough to drown out his thoughts. He could only picture the pond as he dragged himself to shelter, blood trailing behind him. The pond and its bubbling water, its koi fish and their babbling mouths. What was he even doing this—all of this—for?

DEHISCENT

The next few days were cold and wouldn't let up. The frost was thick on the glass of the Zhu house as the humidity from outside coalesced onto the walls and windows. Yi stayed inside for all of it, knowing that even while confined to her home, she still had homework to do.

She watched her parents and grandparents play mahjong while she sat at her cluttered desk, brush pen in hand and wanting instead to join them.

Something rolled onto her foot, rattling along the wood floorboard before hitting her on the heel. She looked down to find a jar, unlabeled and sealed shut. She picked it up, opened the lid, and sighed when she smelled it. "Mama," she said. "Were we out of doubanjiang?"

"Is that another jar?" her mother asked, not bothering to look up from the game.

"Yeah."

"Perfect. Just leave it at your desk, I'll grab it when I start making dinner."

Yi put the jar at the corner of her desk and glanced between her schoolwork and the window. The glass had fogged up, making it difficult to look outside; the frost crystals crawled up the windowpane and covered it like clouds. She gave the jar one last look before packing up her schoolwork and taking it to her room, the clinking of mahjong tiles melding with the rattling of the icy wind against the house.

She laid out her papers and her pen and ink cartridges, sat down in a brief moment of contemplation, then walked past her bed to the windows. She squinted through the frosted glass and then cleared it with her hand, feeling the ice melt away beneath her fingers. And, despite knowing it was useless, she took in a deep breath and searched.

She could see the path she took toward the village before it became too cluttered with old, decaying buildings; it was dusted with snow, more like crystals than they were flakes, tiny shards of ice, balled up in the dead grasses and the sparsely bricked road. The thought of the body made her want to tear into her face with her nails until she bled, but that didn't stop her—she imagined that she could see the corpse anyway, that she could see through the old concrete and wood and metal to spot a figure in the distance, hunched over and frozen solid like a statue. It had been too cold for any decomposition, too dry for the elements to do anything but preserve the body in its huddled, final attempts to stay warm. What would those moments have been? The marks on his face looked like they had been painful, crusted with dried blood. Had he suffered when he died? Had the cold bitten at his wounds and seeped into his core, coating his bones and lungs and heart? Or had he embraced it, letting the cold numb his pain and slow his brain until the dark became endless? Maybe the rain did something, finally let it succumb to its natural fate. Or maybe it just gave it another coating of ice. That would help, probably. Something to slow the decay, the stench—or would the smell be preferred? Maybe then someone else would find it. She listened for the mahjong tiles, the rhythmic mixing and stacking, and a thought occurred to her: what would happen if someone in her family froze to death outside, too? And then another thought: how many others have died out there?

A strong gust of wind assaulted the house. She felt it creak against its frame, felt it strain along its stilts. She took hold of the windowsill for support and heard the wind whistle past, heard the clinking of the mahjong tiles below, heard the violent crashing of the waves.

Winter lasted a week. The polar vortex subsided and the world fell into a foggy limbo as the frost evaporated. The warmth started sluggishly seeping through the wood and terracotta of the house once again.

DEHISCENT

And, over that week, Yi uncovered more food. Mangoes beneath the clean bowls, dried scallops falling out of the faucet, fish—still swimming—in their bathtub. It wasn't an uncommon occurrence for the house to provide food in waves, even when it sensed they weren't in need of any. It was strange to think of it like that. That the house could sense anything. That it somehow knew when they were running low on which ingredients or when they were craving a specific meal. And yet, things appeared from the crevices, rolling out from the baseboards and growing along the bookshelf.

It hadn't mattered to her when she was younger. After all, the house provided, and the Zhu family never had to go hungry.

Now that she was older, she wondered.

When school restarted and the heat picked up again, Yi walked through what seemed like perpetual fog. At first, it was too thick for her to dare stray off her path, filling every alley and collapsed building with a cloud of silvery white. But as she entered the ruins of the town, it receded just enough for her to look into the yawning mouths of the dark buildings, wisps of fog curling out the empty windows and broken doors. It wasn't long before she was taking the same path as the other day, recalling her steps through labyrinthine ruins. It was wet and humid and the air here smelled more like decay than it normally did. She had to be careful not to step into puddles or slide on mud or think too hard about how a body might have decomposed.

Because that was what things did, wasn't it? They rotted and fell apart, just like the buildings of whatever town this had been, so many years ago.

And then she found it: the same crumbling door, the same three walls, the same cracked half-ceiling waiting for a heavy storm to finally come and break it all down. She was surprised the last storm hadn't done so already.

Yi braced herself to look in, peering around the corner sheepishly. Her heart skipped a beat when nothing was there.

She stepped into the room, wary of the collapsing ceiling. She was wrong—there was something here. A pair of boots, soggy and stretched out, strewn on the ground not far from where the body once sat.

Someone had come to do something about him after all. That should've made her feel better, but for some reason it didn't. Her stomach sank further, her skin itched for her to get out of there. Had her father gotten that message to the others? She couldn't think of when, since her family had been holed up in the house the moment it got cold and never left, but maybe someone from the village found him on their own. She hoped that was the answer, but she really didn't want to ask.

Yi walked out backwards—eyes still glued to the abandoned boots—then ran off toward school.

That night, the heat dragged in the humidity, slowly crawling after her as she returned from school; wet, sticky, and suffocating. Wasn't she taught that warmth came with the sun? That the temperature was supposed to drop at night? That rain could wash it away, quench the earth, comfort their sweat-soaked skin? She had a hard time believing any of that—the sun could be bright during blistering cold days and the nights sometimes got so hot and humid that even stepping outside felt like she was being steamed alive. And when the world got like that, Yi stayed far, far away from her windows.

She laid in bed, sweating uncomfortably.

Her room was stuffy, the air thick and sluggish, quiet except for the sound of her breathing. The silence was broken by the sound of shuffling and the click of the front door opening. Yi froze, held her breath, and listened.

A breeze wafted in through the open window, buffeting

DEHISCENT

her with more warm air. She sat up; lying down was only making the heat worse. The steps below continued outside and it was silent enough that she could hear the crunching dead grass underfoot; not even the oppressive humidity could fix how dead and dry the earth had become. For a few moments, that was all she heard and she listened through the rushing of her blood in her ears as the steps faded into the distance, quieting down to soft padding between gentle breezes. Her nerves started as a shaking in her hands and arms and solidified into tears in her eyes because she couldn't stop her thoughts from swirling the same questions over and over and over again: Who in her family was leaving the house in the middle of the night? Why were they even outside?

Yi tried to close her eyes, but she was greeted with the image of the dead supplier. Only, he wasn't dead. Not fully, at least. His face was still torn up and he was bleeding now, steady streams of red oozing from the wounds. The warmth was gone from his deep brown eyes, leaving a pale, greyish tinge that stared back at her, dead, cold, and unseeing. He opened his mouth and tried to speak—

Yi shook herself, trying to push out the image with memories of the house, its lush flora and bright smells.

Minutes passed. Maybe longer. She didn't know how long she'd been pressed against the outer wall of her room when she heard the footsteps return. They fell rhythmically like a metronome, creeping ever closer, followed by a hissing of something being dragged along the dead grass and fine sand. Yi rose to her knees as soundlessly as she could manage, her heart still pounding in her ears as she risked a peek through her window.

She caught a glimpse of her father. And then, she saw the thing on his back.

At first, it looked like no more than a shadow. In the hazy, unlit night, the form of her father had doubled in size, and there were feet trailing behind him in the dirt. The clouds moved with the warm, humid air, and the moon took its chance to shine. Soft, white light filtered down onto dead plants and sallow earth, illuminating her father. He looked ahead, determined, and the body he carried was limp.

Yi didn't know why she was crying, she just was. Tears welled in her eyes as her thoughts caught up with her emotions. Who did that body belong to? What was her father doing? She took in the sight one last time before her father reached the steps to their house, the body hunched over his back like a growth. Its hair was matted to its head, its arms wrapped around her father's neck, her dad holding it in place by its wrists. He stopped for a moment to open the door, then dragged the body into their home.

Yi slid to the floor, too terrified to make a noise, and waited.

And listened.

She listened for the quiet thumping of the corpse's ankles hitting the steps of the staircase behind her father's footfalls.

She listened, trying to mark his movement within the house.

To the creaking of the stairs that led to the attic and the soft thuds as they ascended.

Her heart dropped once she realized where they were going. She trailed the sound upward, to the ceiling of her room.

This was not the first time Yi heard movement in the attic. She had always thought that the house was simply creaking; it was old, after all, and it sat precariously close to the edge of a cliff, battered by tempest winds and waters, the ocean lapping at it with each beckoning tide. The Zhu house, with its aging wood and terracotta, should not have held on for as long as it has.

The shuffling continued above her for a few moments before her father's footsteps finally returned to the door and down the stairs. She heard him through the walls as he entered his bedroom, carefully turning the door handle to close it with as little noise as possible.

Yi took a breath.

DEHISCENT

In the darkness beneath her bed, something moved. She jumped and fell onto her side, swallowing a yelp of surprise. A box emerged in front of her, peeking out into the moonlight; cardboard and blue. Why was the house giving her something now?

She reached out and pulled it into the light. It was a small box of tissues. She plucked one out with a shaky hand and wiped away the tears.

The next morning, Yi was quiet.

Because she didn't know what else to do about last night.

Because, unless she had dreamt it all, there was a body in the house and her father was the one who brought it in.

It had been a while since she'd thought about the attic. It was another part of the house, and just like the rest of it, she didn't think too hard about it. The house was weird and there was no point in trying to really question it, none of it made sense anyway. But now, well. Did her father murder a man? Why else did he drag a body all the way home? Maybe he wasn't dead—but what else could it be?

There were too many questions and Yi didn't want answers to any of them.

Yi ate her breakfast in silence, feigning no change in temperament or suspicions, though she remembered the tiger she'd imagined in the attic and suddenly she felt a lot worse about where that body went. As far as her family was aware she was just begrudgingly doing all her homework before the weather lightened up enough to go to school. Like any other day. So she prodded at her bowl of juk with a stick of youtiao, swirling the meat and white pepper and scallions as though very interested in the buoyancy of rice cooked down into soft, creamy porridge. She could barely keep her eyes open, but she didn't want to sleep. Sleep was where her memories came alive and she wanted to avoid reliving last night as much as possible.

"Ah, Amuy," said her grandfather from the other side of the kitchen table. "You look tired. Did you sleep?"

"Yeah," she lied. "I'm okay, Ayeh." Another lie.

"You know . . . you don't have to wake up so early if you don't want to." He grinned at her, like he was sharing a sly secret between the two of them. Her parents would've insisted she not sleep in anyway, even if she had permission from Ayeh. "Let me get you some tea."

Yi nodded. She was always grateful for the tea in her house and its ever-present place in her life and she was starting to realize that it was probably because it meant she had an abundance of clean water—not so full of minerals as to ruin the taste or require any filtration to remove all the gunk that she'd seen in the village. Clean water and the tea itself, somehow, all thanks to the house. And the house provided multiple kinds of tea too; there were oolongs and black teas and green teas and herbals, too much for her family to drink but forbidden to share anyway. She still thought about it, though. The idea of taking a bunch of tea leaves—however useless they were to the villagers—snuck its way into her thoughts again as her grandfather placed a cup of milk tea—milk! actual milk! another thing she took for granted—in front of her. Maybe that's what she was going to do today.

Here's what Yi had to work with:

Whatever she brought to school needed to be small, shareable, and in enough quantity that no one missed out. *(note to self: how many kids are in my class again?)*

It needed to be mundane and common enough so that it wouldn't raise any suspicions in either her classmates or her teachers *(pay closer attention to what everyone has at school)*

At the same time, it needed to be at least a little special and interesting, not that she wanted to show off, but she still wanted things to be meaningful. *(I like candy, and fruit, and having fresh meat, but it's all special to them, isn't it?)*

She sat at her desk wracking her brain for something that fit the criteria. She wasn't even sure they'd accept gifts, like what would they think of snacks or candy or lunch from her? She was probably too much that weird kid who lived outside of the village, too much of an outsider to ever be part of the group. She hoped they just saw her as the quiet kid, and she was fairly sure no one actively disliked her. But even then she admitted it'd probably be a little weird. She'd need to make it less weird, somehow. And that probably meant it was a good idea to wait just a little bit longer.

When her father passed down the hallway toward the kitchen, Yi pretended to be very interested in the homework she had barely touched, sitting open on the desk before her. She felt her pulse quicken and she tried to control her breathing to keep the panic from rising like her heartbeat. But it was hot and it was humid and the panic came anyway; her Baba, who always let her have first pick at the toys or tech or fabrics he scavenged, who was always on the lookout for old cartoons that could be played on the CRTs so she would have something to remind her of the world that was and could have been, who comforted her when she had nightmares and pretended to literally chase the bad dreams out of the house.

That Baba.

Yi couldn't stop thinking he might also be a murderer.

And if he was—could she tell anyone? What could she even do? She couldn't tell her grandparents, she couldn't tell her mother. Her teacher? The other kids? Where would she live? Who would take her in? No, there weren't any good options for Yi. She could only stay in her house with the knowledge that there was a dead body in her attic and she couldn't tell anyone about it.

Sorting through who she could and could not trust made her feel very, very small. She was helpless to do anything. She couldn't just abandon her family, they would never forgive her and she'd never forgive herself, and so, she had to watch. And wait. And learn, hopefully. There must have been more, she kind of hoped there was more. Because why would her father bring the body *in?* If he wanted to dispose of it, wasn't the cliff better? Drop the thing into the ocean, let the waters crash the corpse against the rocks and turn it into a mass of flesh and bones and—

There was a slow but steady plopping sound coming from the cabinet. She jumped as she heard the mass of gingko fruit falling from the top of the shelf and for a brief moment she just stared. This wasn't the first time this had happened to her and it definitely wouldn't be the last time she sat here doing her work only to be interrupted by the cabinet gingkos, longing to spread their potential offspring into the world. Yi took a breath and steadied herself. She was kind of grateful, honestly. She needed to be careful not to do it again. Even though, well, it was tempting. Because really, what else could she do?

The house shook a little again, just the wall behind her this time, and Yi turned around to see the little patch of strawberries starting to bloom; small, white flowers dotted the panel of wood covered in nascent strawberry leaves. She smiled. It had been a while since she had any strawberries. She buried the thought before it came; strawberries would *definitely* be too suspicious.

After hours of staring at and memorizing her vocabulary sets, Yi gave up and glued herself to the CRT in the living room. She could feel the static coming off it through the humidity, prickling the air in front of her. She was watching some live-action drama she vaguely recognized as an adaptation of the folklore in the stories her parents would read to her, even if they weren't exactly the same and the many newly-introduced character dynamics felt unfamiliar and superfluous. She didn't really care. It was hot and she was sweaty, and the people in the CRT lived in a landscape that looked unattainably foreign. She tried to focus on learning from the subtitles that flashed past instead of thinking too hard about how the world used to be green and lush and full of life.

Eventually, she gave up. She lay with her back on the floor, the humidity pressing down on her chest and filling her lungs. She could barely breathe; it felt thick enough to grab with her hands and pull over her head like a sheet. The CRT buzzed away, louder than usual as though clinging to the moisture in the air. She wanted to join the people on the CRT, bathing in a river that was clean and glistening. The scene changed quickly—no longer were they resting by the river, they were being attacked by bandits.

A bottle rolled into her arm, cool against her bare skin. She sat up and turned it over in her hands. It was filled with an attractive, pale orange liquid and the glass bottle itself dripped with condensation. She unscrewed the lid and gave it a whiff; it was sweet and fruity in a way she couldn't quite describe. Drinking it felt the same. She was pretty sure she'd never had the fruit used to make it, but it was sweet and fruity and refreshing in the way she imagined the river on the CRT to be. It was over way too quick.

But Yi, sticky and exhausted by the heat, needed something else. A single bottle of juice just wasn't enough.

So she wandered back to her room, and then to the bathroom, and rolled the die that was her shower. She never knew when the water would be cold or practically hot enough to make tea from. And, apparently, her parents didn't either. But she tried it anyway, because everything outside sucked. Sometimes she wondered if the water in the ocean was any better, but even on a calm day she couldn't imagine wading into the billions of tiny, dead creatures that littered the water.

The shower rattled to life and Yi was immediately greeted by a gust of cool air. She stood next to it for a few minutes, letting the cold water wick away the heat around her, before stripping down for a long, cold shower. The air was clearer here and it helped her clear her mind, too. She closed her eyes, water dripping down her face, and her thoughts wandered back to the attic.

Suddenly, the cold felt deeply, deeply unwelcome.

Yi hated that she was excited to go back to school—who got excited to go to *school?*—but she was starting to suffocate being at home with her parents. No, that wasn't it, was it? She was just avoiding Baba, only Baba—she still enjoyed her time with her grandparents or helping her mother prepare the wash bins for cleaning the garments meant for the village. It was the caution she had around her father that made her feel small, trapped. Not just being around him, either. She didn't want to *think* about him, didn't want to look too closely at her memories of him, didn't want to pick up all the clues that she might've missed after all these years. School was a welcome distraction. School was time away.

She headed out early, said good-bye to her parents and grandparents and braced herself for the sun. She gave herself a plan: talk to the other kids and figure out what she could bring to share out to her classmates. There, that was something to do. Something that wasn't dwelling on all the death she'd seen lately. Two bodies in her life already. At least, she was pretty sure it was two.

She sighed. Even with school, she was still thinking about it.

The square was full of kids and their parents when she arrived. Normally, she was too late to catch the adults dropping off their kids, if they didn't just let them walk to the courtyard themselves. It was nice seeing the parents of her classmates, though she didn't really get why. Maybe it was the small glimpse it gave her of life here beyond her school, beyond Xie Laoshi and the suppliers, beyond the occasional personnel she passed in the old library. Or maybe she just liked the commotion, where people felt like people, even in the desolation of Fengxian and its surrounding infrastructure. The crowd here wasn't lining up for rations, wasn't waiting for scraps of a long-dead civilization; this was like the sort of normal she only saw on the shows she watched. She wondered how it felt for everyone else.

Yi wandered in awkwardly. The other kids hadn't started settling into their seats yet and she didn't want to start class yet either, so she made her way through the moms and dads giving pep talks and stern warnings to please pay attention, at least until the end of day. She hadn't seen most of the parents here before, other than the brief glimpses she got on the occasional days she was actually here to see those rations get distributed. She was old enough to understand the irony; her parents wanted her to come to school, to socialize with the other kids, and all she did was avoid them if she could. But, what else was she supposed to do? What could she even talk to them about?

Someone called her name and it took her a moment to even register it. She tried to put on a smile as Qianfan, next to his mom, waved her down. Yi waved back and was inclined to leave it at that, but she knew she was going to need to befriend people *eventually* and frankly, the sooner the better. She hoped it'd help her mood.

Qianfan's mother frowned sympathetically. "Your parents don't come by much, do they?" she asked. Yi noticed the shirt she was wearing and recognized the red-brown floral and polka dot pattern from when it made its way into her dad's bag of scraps.

"Just to drop stuff off," Yi replied. *Like your shirt,* she wanted to say. "The house is a lot of work to take care of."

That was the trade-off: live safely and comfortably in the Zhu family house at the expense of being able to openly befriend anyone else. She settled for the half-lie.

"I can imagine," said Qianfan's mom, though Yi could feel the undertone of disapproval. "You're lucky to have a house that survived everything."

"It's a lot to take care of," she repeated, mumbling.

Qianfan piped up, his smile pushing the baby fat of his cheeks like over-stuffed cushions. "Ruzhang and Wei and Zijie and Ziqi and me are gonna try out this basketball we found! A-After school, of course." He watched his mom out of the corner of his eyes, cautious that he was within the boundaries of acceptable for a well-behaved student and child. His mom smiled—genuinely, this time. She had the same round face and shallow-set eyes, but there was age in them, dark bags from life and stress that Qianfan hadn't yet developed himself.

"You should join them," she said to Yi. "Qianfan thinks you need friends."

"You don't need to tell her that!"

Yi almost said no. It was at the tip of her tongue, her instinctive response to any questions about or of her in any way. *My parents want me home, my parents need my help, I'm sorry, I'm just not allowed to hang out with the other kids.* She'd practised those excuses so many times, they rolled out before thinking. But this time, she forced herself to agree, stitching together the new information Qianfan gave her: she knew everyone he mentioned, could even pick out Ruzhang and Wei and the two Liu siblings Zijie and Ziqi, but she had no idea that they were all friends. She'd never bothered to pay attention. She felt guilty about that now.

"Where do you want to go with it?' she asked. "What does it do?"

Qianfan shrugged. "I dunno. It's bouncy. Should be fun to throw at each other." He grinned, ear-to-ear, like the idea of whipping a ball at his friends was the most delight he'd had in years. Which Yi knew wasn't true. Qianfan gave that exact same grin when he challenged the rest of the class to a race around the village. That was one of the few activities Yi joined in on. She was normally here on days with decent weather anyway and no one was interested in talking when you're running at full speed.

Yi tuned out the rest. Qianfan's mom was telling him to be patient with Yi and to eat all of his lunch while she stared past them both, to where the Liu siblings stood with their identical haircuts, curling inward at the ears and cut straight across except for the bangs above the eyes, making them look years younger than they actually were. Yi was fairly sure Zijie was her age and his sister a year younger; they were the only siblings in the village who were less than a few years close in age and Yi was pretty sure it was because their father helped with the communications to the facilities outside the village. It meant he knew who to contact in an emergency like childbirth and how to do so quickly. Yi remembered her mom mentioning something about planning and she also remembered wondering, at the time, if her parents had to plan around her birth too, or if the Zhu house helped with that too. Now, the question expanded: Did her parents have siblings? Her grandparents?

The Liu siblings' dad waved them off as the kids started to gather for class, grabbing their carpet and tarp scraps and settling in front of Xie Laoshi. Even Qianfan ran off, his mother already long gone. But Yi's focus was on Zijie and Ziqi's dad, who—in his clothes made from scraps like everyone else—was joined by another man as they walked toward the old library, this one wearing a crumpled and worn jacket with a logo on it, blue instead of green. She couldn't make out what it said but it had more structure to the collar and shoulders than the uniform the suppliers wore, and she was sure it was more than just another scrap from around the old city. When the man pulled out a jumble of electronics from the inside pocket of his jacket, Yi decided he was probably working on something with the communications or maybe it was the air conditioning in the building. She was barely around enough to see what needed repairs, if they could be repaired at all. Which was sad. She'd never had to worry about anything like that at all. She barely knew the fullness of people's lives in Fengxian.

Was that how her dad felt? Growing up in the Zhu house away from everyone else, just as she did?

Yi sucked in a breath remembering her dad and the corpse and the attic. Maybe that wasn't how her dad felt. Maybe that wasn't how he felt about the people of Fengxian at all.

She felt a tug at her arm and almost jumped; next to her stood Qianfan, who looked at her sheepishly. "Come on," he whispered as though trying to warn her. "We're starting."

"R-Right," Yi stammered. "School."

The next day was rainy, heavily so; the storm overhead poured acidic rain, grim and violent. Yi flinched every time the wind rammed into the side of the house, the bones of the Zhu house moaning and creaking. Normally, on days like this, Yi stuck close to her family because she hated being alone with the elements, vulnerable and small, even so far away from the outside walls. But she couldn't pretend like everything was normal—she wanted to, she tried, it'd been days since her dad dragged a dead body into their house but she was pretty sure her anxiety was getting worse. She avoided her Baba, spent as little time as she could in the same room as him, kept to herself, pretended to be busy with homework or very invested in the shows on the CRT. She'd even started a small pile of fabric scraps in her room; *I'm gonna start helping*, she told her mom. *I might as well, right?* Still, every time she saw her dad, she panicked a little.

Yi was curled up on the couch by the CRT, which flickered, staticky, every time thunder struck overhead, while her parents played daiyi at the kitchen table. She glanced over; the cards were stacked in a tall pile between them. Her mother was winning, with the smaller hand between her and Baba. Her father brushed off his impending loss with a smile that grew and grew, just as his hand did, with each passing turn. Yi wished she could just see her father as her father, that her dad was just playing cards with her mom, that nothing was any different than last month, last year. But she couldn't. The image of her father dragging a corpse into her home was burned into her mind, and she couldn't work out if her mom knew about it too, which bugged her when she thought too much about it—how could she just *sit there if she did?* Then again, was anything actually different? Maybe her mom's always known. Maybe her dad's been picking up corpses for longer than Yi knew. She really hated that idea.

Yi peeled herself off the couch. She couldn't stay here any longer, everything felt suffocating and tight and prickly along her skin. She took in a deep breath to steady herself and wandered upstairs, curtly letting her parents know she'd be studying in her room.

But she wasn't going to her room.

The stairs leading to the attic felt cold and mundane. This was the only spot in the house where the plants felt artificial, unnatural. Elsewhere in the house, the plants felt like they were part of her home; integrated like the furniture and interacting like family. But here, here the plants reached out, evenly interspersed. The branches of clean white jasmine and bright red goji felt like they were guarding the attic with a sacred duty.

She flicked on the light switch and the light above her, at the bottom of the stairs, flicked on in turn. She pictured her father the other night, dragging up a body, replaying the thud of the corpse's feet hitting the steps in the middle of the night. She whipped her head around one last time, making sure that she was alone before tiptoeing up the steps.

When she reached the top, she paused, holding her

breath and listening to the sounds of her family below her. The rain had started to lighten up to a gentle, rhythmic patter against the roof, and below was nothing but the idle chatter of her grandparents and parents. There was the shuffling of cards, the shuffling of chairs, the shuffling of tiles. She sighed, relieved—they had started a new mahjong game. Good.

Slowly, she opened the door.

On the other side, pale, weak light streamed into the attic from the far windows; soft from the expanse of ocean beyond, filtered through the scattering rain clouds. It filled the room with a careful touch, as though gently painting each dead body with a wash of grey-white as they hung by their ankles from the rafters. The sun, reaching through the house, distantly from the storm, welcomed Yi into the forbidden.

Without thinking, Yi closed the door behind her.

The attic wasn't the cluttered mess her parents led her to believe. Instead, it was bare, the plain wooden bones of the house holding the bodies from the rafters. There were so many of them, rows upon rows upon rows, hung by rope tied to their ankles. Their dead eyes—if they still had eyes—stared back at her.

Yi expected a stinking pile of corpses for some reason, and even the tiger made sense to her suddenly, and she could picture this space filled with the blood and viscera of a hungry animal's maul, but instead these were neatly arranged in rows of three, lacking any smell of decay. Everything about what she saw in front of her was wrong. Still, mutilated bodies, packed tightly enough to be shoulder to shoulder with each other, without any foul smells ever wafting through the wood from the attic. There wasn't even blood, nothing to give away its contents, but there should have been *something*, she should have *known*.

The attic, still, was faintly musty—although she thought that was probably just the wood—and dust floated along on streams of light from the window. She stood stock still, not daring to move. Would they hear her downstairs? Would the floor of the attic creak? She dragged her eyes back up, to face the mutilation she'd caught a peek at—one dead body was already a lot to wrap her head around. An attic full of them . . .

There were entire parts missing from them. Even under their clothes. But their parts were too cleanly removed, and the lack of blood made her rule out her father. There were no tools here, just rope. Bodies and rope, and the bodies were barely whole. In fact, most of them had become slack-jawed, if they had jaws left at all. Others were missing limbs or lips or eyelids, and the bodies farthest from the entrance seemed to have their flesh melted off. They'd been reduced to bone and cartilage, skeletons somehow still held together, and clothes hung to dry from the rafters. The closer they were to the entrance, the more flesh remained on their frames. Somewhere in the middle were the brightest—their faces bright red with criss-crossing lines of fascia and air-dried muscle tissue. Teeth stared back at her just as much as the eyes did.

Yi felt nauseous, lightheaded. Bile rose in her throat and she swallowed it down, slowly stepping toward the centre of the attic, ignoring every prick of fear that cascaded down her neck. She walked past the newest corpse, searching for the man she found dead from the cold, huddled in on himself inside of an abandoned building. It didn't take long—he wasn't far behind the latest body, his arms still curled, his legs still bent. His skin had faded from his face and down his arms, leaving the bright red muscle exposed to the air. She only caught the blueish tint of his skin from the exposed calves where gravity pulled down on his pant legs.

She stopped herself there. She was so close—too close—to touching the bodies, to feeling what they'd become inside of her home. Were they wet? Cold? Warm from the constant heat waves that slammed into the Zhu home? She didn't want to think about when her dad must've gotten these other bodies, didn't even want to imagine who they had once been.

DEHISCENT

She wanted to claw under her skin, scratch at things she didn't have the words for, but she felt them all churning inside, bubbling up and over, red and hot and swollen. The nausea didn't go away; it followed her out the attic and into her room.

Yi ran a hot shower, stepping into the scalding water, and scrubbed her skin clean. Water poured out the rattling showerhead and she stood under the shaky stream, hoping that the warmth would calm her nerves. It did, a little. Warmth for her muscles and steady, white noise for her thoughts.

A ball rolled out from the bottles of soap and shampoo, small and chalky but pleasant-smelling. It fell into the tub by her feet and the steam filled the shower with unknown green scents. It was bright and earthy and fresh in a way she had only ever imagined the world could have smelled like before.

And, despite the reprieve, her eyes drifted upward to the attic.

The Zhu family house had been built in two stages—the older, bottom floors were in the traditional style of Chinese homes of some era whose name had long been lost to history while the second floor and the attic had been attached later on, bearing the tell-tale signs of 19th century European influence. Once, it belonged to a civil servant, then an exporter, then a series of Zhu family men who grew more and more eclectic the longer they tended to the house, some ashamed of their duty, some thoroughly engaged. None of this Yi knew, mostly she could never figure out what to make of it and she frankly never thought to care. This was her home, this was where she and her family had lived for generations. It didn't matter that the house was old and confused in its materials and architecture. It just *was*, and Yi accepted it as a fact of life.

Now, though, Yi had a sinking feeling she knew why the attic was built. She wondered where they kept the bodies before the house's expansion.

She imagined the halls of the main floor strung up with bodies at intervals from the wooden beams, like the bowels of the house laid bare and open, the inner viscera exposed, hallowed and serene. And even though she didn't exactly know what the bodies did for the house, she could guess, she was old enough to piece it together. And she hated it. After all, her family had lived here for generations and—no, she didn't even want to think about it.

Yi sat with her back against her bedroom wall. She needed a distraction—badly. Her arms shook and she was blinking back years and she felt like she was going to burst if she didn't do something to take her mind off it. So she pulled down her homework from her desk and practised her vocabulary. And then her math. And then when the numbers and the writing practise started to merge together and she was doing arithmetic in the spaces of big, sparsely-written characters, she closed her eyes and let out a long sigh.

Something small and hard fell from her desk with a *plunk*. It rolled onto her, wrapped in thin, brown paper. It was only about as big as her thumb, round and hard, and when she began to unwrap it, more came down onto her like hail, battering her from all sides.

Yi covered her head with her hands until it subsided. And when it did, it was suddenly very, very quiet. For a moment, her heart pounding in her ears was all she heard.

Her mother called from downstairs, her voice tinny through the wood. "Yi, what was that?!"

"Nothing!" Yi cried back.

She examined her surroundings, taking in all the little balls wrapped in wrinkled brown paper. It was certainly not nothing. She was going to need to do something about all this.

"Yi!" her mother cried again.

DEHISCENT

"I-It's nothing! My pencils fell—that's it!"

Yi half expected her mother to come up and catch her with the mess and, more awkwardly, the fact that she had been sitting on the floor on the brink of a crisis. So when she didn't, and there were no other steps ascending to the second floor, Yi tried to forced the blood back down from her ears and cheeks and turned her attention to the little ball in her hand. She unwrapped it, revealing a layer of clear, bright red crystal covering something equally red but spotted on the inside. It was sticky and smelled strongly of sweets and Yi put it to her lips and took a bite.

The candy tasted faintly familiar, like a relative of the strawberry, and the word *hawthorn* popped into her head. That's what it was on the inside, she realized. She'd had this fruit before, many years ago. But she'd never had it so thoroughly covered in hardened sugar. It was a little tough to bite through but she liked it. She certainly liked it enough that she ate three and, in looking around at the mess of wrapped candied hawthorn on her bedroom floor, she considered throwing them all into a bag and handing them out at school. She did the first bit and left it next to her schoolbag by the foot of her bed. She was still undecided on the second one, though. She wanted to do something. She *should* do something, the answer literally fell onto her lap— but how?

In the mornings before she went to school, Yi watched her father with a quiet, maddening suspicion. And then that suspicion moved to her mother then her grandfather and then slowly, finally, reluctantly, to her grandmother. Because, she realized, there was no way the others didn't know. No possible way this house had stayed in her family this long without that secret whispered among its inhabitants over the generations and there was no way she could confront them about it, nothing else she could do but continue being their child. She'd worked it out by now too—the disappearing flesh, the impossibility of the Zhu house—but she hadn't accepted it just yet. No, that wasn't true, either. She had accepted that this was the way the house worked, but she didn't like it, didn't want this to be her life, didn't think she'd ever be okay with it. It made her realize she was more afraid than she was angry or sad that her memories of this house, and the memories of her family, were forever coloured by the knowledge of the bodies hanging in the attic, silent and swaying as the house was hit by the wind. The bottles that rattled out from the edges of the Zhu house made her jump now, as though the house was watching her and wanted to speak.

She even left on the days that were hotter than she usually would, not that being inside the house was any better. If anything, she couldn't stand being in there with the humidity circulating like dead air and the actual, tangible dead things looming over her head. It didn't matter that she couldn't see them. She felt them. And on the days when it was particularly sunny, she turned on her heels to look back at the Zhu family house as she walked toward the path to school. Her eyes always drifted toward the roof, imagining the wood and shingles turning translucent like the corpses' skin and she pictured them, tied by the ankles and hung like choy put out to dry. The rest of the house stood as it always had—imposing on its stilts, misshapen and confused—with the dust around it picking up with the wind. Sea-spray hit her face, and it smelled a bit like the thing in the shower: bright, fresh, and earthy. Not quite as green, though. That bit was hard to explain.

When Yi got to the courtyard, the kids were still killing time before they were summoned to class. Ruzhang—tall, disheveled, and outgrowing his clothes—waved her over. He was with Wei and Qianfan, who were busy bouncing the basketball on the ground between them. Normal kid things,

Yi thought. Just like those shows she watched and absolutely nothing like her life. And then: *it could be*. They didn't have play structures or elaborate toys or some great evil to join together to destroy; it was more like those dramas from a time even longer ago, where there wasn't much to play other than the things they could scrounge together with their own hands and the few tools they had available to them. Just without any of the lush greens of a world still in balance.

Wei almost knocked Qianfan in the face with the ball, earning them all a sharp warning from Xie Laoshi from the edge of the courtyard. "Sorry," said Wei, picking up the basketball. "It's bouncier than I expected."

"Did you get it inflated?" asked Yi.

"Yeah," Ruzhang replied. "The electricity's sort of working again in the school."

Qianfan grinned as though he hadn't almost completely gotten battered in the face with a ball bigger than the size of his head. "You know what that means!" he exclaimed. "Air conditioning!"

They filed into the old library, the kids chatting amongst themselves as they usually did when they got the chance to be indoors with working machinery that gave them cool, dehumidified air. The administrative staff waved and smiled as they passed, the adults of Fengxian wanting to give the kids hospitality they deserved, the sort that they could've gotten elsewhere had the world not lost its own, innate hospitality generations ago. Yi wondered if anyone even remembered the world of the before, or if their parents remembered any of it either; what life was like before the planet seemingly collapsed, before the chaos that ensued destroyed cities and continents both. She wasn't even sure they'd talk about it if they did. Even Xie Laoshi didn't speak of the collapse in any great detail, and that was her job, in a way. Teach the kids about the world around them. Surely that would include the collapse, but when she did talk about it, it made Yi think that she, too, wanted to know more. Like she'd been shut out of that knowledge from the start. Not even the adults here learned about it—it was a different generation's trauma, important enough to pass down the causes of the collapse and complain plenty that the solutions came too late, but they'd never actually discussed the death and disasters that ravaged the world. Nothing much more than *It happened*. Seeing the extent of the ruins that stood as empty exoskeletons of once-great cities, Yi could guess at the devastation. She was probably never going to fully grasp it, and she figured no singular person could.

One of the men, a mechanic in the loose uniform of the suppliers, walked past with Zijie and Ziqie's dad. He was holding a box full of tools and various circuitry. Yi only heard part of the conversation before she was shuffled into class:

" . . . but people have been going missing," the mechanic was saying. "I just hope we can keep things going reliably. Maybe it'll keep people safe."

"How is Shanghai?"

"Better. Not great, but better."

"People missing up there too?"

"It's the *weather*—we can't expect that absolutely no one gets caught in the changes."

"The generators would be good to prioritize then, keeps people indoors where it's . . . "

Safe, Yi finished in her head. Comfortable, safe, protected from the elements. Unlike the supplier she ran into weeks ago. She hated that she couldn't tell for certain if the other bodies in her attic fell to the same fate. Because that meant her father might have had a hand in their deaths and it didn't matter how long she sat on that hypothetical: she was fairly sure she loved her father even through all this and she deeply resented the idea that he might be a murderer. Fairly sure. What a stupid thing to even have to worry about. It made her stomach feel sharply empty.

DEHISCENT

Yi took her seat and her hand brushed the bag full of candied hawthorn inside her backpack. She froze. She forgot she had stuffed them in there and, by the feel of it, they only survived the trip by melting and leaking and turning into one giant, saccharinely sweet candy ball with many hawthorns inside. Brown paper wrapping and all. Gross. Also probably impossible to pass around. She'd have to do something about that after, like chipping the candy apart with a knife in order to salvage anything to eat. Definitely not something she wanted to do there. Her books already had a tinge of red candy along the edges, but she wiped her fingers on it anyway, trying to clean off the sugar that clung to her skin. When the stickiness had sufficiently dulled, she pulled out her notebook and pretended the bag didn't smell faintly of fruit.

The next heatwave came with dry, hot wind. She watched from inside as the dust picked up, turning into clouds. It billowed and roiled, obscuring her view. Everything around the Zhu house became a dull, yellow haze with shadowy forms dancing within it. A knot grew in her throat as she watched the world fade in and out, picturing herself wandering out there in the storm. What would hit her first: the heat or the dust? Would it coat her lungs, her mouth and her throat? Would it cake on her eyes and shrivel them dry? And then she wondered: Was anyone out there right now? Did they get caught in the weather? Did they have anything to protect them? If they died out there, near the Zhu family house, would they join the others in the attic?

A jar rattled onto her desk, filled with a clear, somewhat milky liquid. She picked it up gingerly and turned it over, trying to hold it to the light to examine its contents, watching the liquid inside move like water. She twisted the cap open. It smelled of fruit and sweet, and she took a drink. *Coconut*, she thought. She didn't know how she knew that—she was fairly sure she'd never had coconut before—but it parched the dryness in her throat that she had imagined into place.

The house always seemed to know what they wanted, regardless of words spoken aloud; it knew, somehow, the way that bodies knew what foods to crave when they're deficient of certain nutrients. Yi understood this, emphatically and instinctively, but she still wondered *how* and—more importantly—why? The house provided. Maybe it didn't matter.

There was rain again, brief and heavy, but the landscape seemed to inhale its long-awaited breath. It wanted to lap and soak, to be drenched until the water sufficiently reached the long-dead roots of plants and the hearty, resilient microorganisms awaiting their chance to finally return.

It lasted five minutes, but the rain came down in sheets. Lightning battled the clouds overhead, bright, rolling, and filled with energy.

Somewhere, in the outskirts of a once-sprawling city, a mechanic jostled a generator into action and a once-dead electrical grid sprang to life along its patchworked lines. The electricity in the air was bristling.

The rain had mostly slowed to a lazy spittle from the sky onto the roof, sliding in equally lazy waterdrops of the shingles to the ground. Yi waited at the top of the stairs, hugging her knees. It was almost bedtime and the lower level of the Zhu house was quiet, with hushed shuffling and murmured words. There was no reason to be, but the night carried with it a blanket of muffled calm. She forced her nerves to still.

Amah and Ayeh came up first. They smiled at her and

exchanged goodnights and headed straight to their bedroom, closing the door behind them. She almost wanted to follow their lead, go straight to bed and forget all about this. But she had to ask. She had to know, even if she didn't want to.

Her mother came up next and gave her a quick "Go to bed!" before doing exactly that. Yi ignored her and stayed where she was, as much as she wanted to listen.

"Yi."

There was Baba. One hand on the rail, halfway up the steps. He was smiling softly.

Yi's heart rate spiked. She wanted to give in and cry because all she could think of was the corpse, the attic, and her dad, and she couldn't figure out how to wrangle the memory of the father who raised her onto the memory of her father with a dead body, dragging it into the house. He felt like a stranger to her.

"Is there something wrong?" he asked. "Did you want to tell me something?"

Go to bed, was what Yi was hearing. *Go to bed because these secrets aren't for you.*

"I, uh . . . " Yi stammered. She swallowed and tried again. "What's in the attic?"

Her dad frowned. "Storage. Lots of old pictures and useless junk from everyone who lived here before us. You know, old family heritage stuff. Except it's *really old*." His tone lightened at that, just a hair.

She breathed in deeply, unused to pressing her parents. She was afraid of the answer and she knew it. "Okay but . . . is it?" Her heart pounded in her ears.

Her dad put both arms over the rail, leaning his body against it. "Yi, what do you want to know?"

"I want to know what's in the attic!"

"I just told you. It's useless junk. Piles of it."

"Then why can't I go up there?" She caught him before he could respond, his mouth half-open. "How does this house know?" she blurted.

Her father pressed his lips together, suddenly serious. "That's a secret. A family secret."

"I'm family!"

"You aren't old enough."

"Baba. Baba please—"

"I'll tell you when you're older."

The tears finally welled up in Yi's eyes. She took a shaky breath and forced them down, adjusting her composure to keep her voice steady. "I've been up there," she said, louder than she anticipated. "I—I saw them. The people." This time, the words came out quiet.

She looked up at her father's face, expecting him to be angry. Angry that she had somehow violated the trust of her family, that she had trespassed in the very house she lived in. But instead, he nodded. And he sighed.

When the silence dragged on, she continued: "It's just—it's been bad outside. This past week. Everything. I-I wasn't sure if you were going to . . . y'know."

"I think we've been okay," he said quietly. "The house hasn't been slowing down."

"Baba—"

"That's what it does. It's what it needs." He gave her a small, sad smile. "This house . . . needs people. And in return, it looks after us."

"How long has this been happening? Did you—?"

Her father shook his head and she felt a wash of relief. Relief with a mighty dosage of confusion. "I've never killed anyone," he said. "I was taught to look for . . . scraps. And it happens a lot now." He climbed up the rest of the stairs and sat next to her. "I think this house has been around long enough that there was a time it didn't need to do this. Or at least, not as often. There's no dedicated grounds for our family's dead. One probably lasted a lifetime when the world was a better place."

Yi didn't know what else to say. She also didn't know how she wanted to feel about this—what if he was still lying? She bristled at the thought of those bodies and this house, her *home*. Everything it did to protect them, everything she ate, smelled, held, wanted to *share*—it came from the house and it came from those bodies. What did she even want anymore? She was suddenly very, very tired.

"Go to sleep," said Baba. He patted her on the knee before getting up and going to bed himself.

Yi sat and waited.

The bodies hanging from the rafters disappeared slowly. The bones of the oldest corpses had finally started to fade away, and she noticed a finger bone vanished every time the waves below rattled the house. She wondered how much longer it could keep up.

Was this worth it? To be sustained by death, to share that sustenance with others despite their origin? It had always been forbidden before but now it was forbidden in a way that made Yi's stomach turn and her arms go numb. She'd lived this her entire life, she reminded herself. This is all she'd ever known.

The body of the supplier she'd found frozen to death had lost the skin from his legs, and exposed muscle peeked out from beneath the pant legs. Then, it disappeared more, seemingly shrinking upward toward his ankle as a bottle of dark mushroom soy rolled out from the walls.

She picked it up and raised it to the light. A deep, brown liquid sloshed inside the bottle. She popped open the lid and gave it a taste; it was earthy, salty, and slightly sweet.

The house provided.

Her eyes wandered across the corpses in the rafters—nine of them, she had counted, and there had been more in the past. They hung curiously; skeletons held together despite their lack of flesh. The wind whistled as it rushed past the Zhu house. She felt the wood rattle and watched another finger bone fade away from existence.

The house provided—what else did it do?

It was hot and humid but Yi went to school anyway, falling into the kind of excitement that she felt like she was *supposed* to have about school. Not the learning part, that bit was never fun, but excitement at seeing her friends, to talk to them about, well, anything. It was energizing—she didn't care about the weather. And, in her bag, was a singular candy. The only one she managed to salvage after stickying her hands with sugar and fruit. She wrapped it in some of that brown wax paper she'd found, pretended not to care about the way the wax melted into the sugar, and stuffed it into the little pocket at the front of her bag. She didn't know what she was going to do about it, she just did it. It felt good, but it also terrified her. Suspicion that her family was hoarding goods was one thing. An attic full of corpses was something else entirely. Which corpse did the candy come from? What part of its body? She tried not to think about it. Everything was just so profoundly unfair that Yi didn't know how to balance her feelings. She decided she wanted to help. She didn't want to be too hard on the *how*.

It made her head spin.

Yi was greeted by a very excited Qianfan. She grinned back—his excitement was contagious but it was *good*, it *felt good*—and Qianfan ran over to share the news.

"Air conditioning!" he cried. "Not just the school building, either! I figured you didn't know that because you don't live here with us . . . "

Give him the candy, Yi.

"Yeah . . . I can tell." She smiled, watching the others standing together nearer to Xie Laoshi, waiting to see if they'd come join them. "I'm kinda jealous . . . my house is so hot." She pulled off her bag and held it in front of her. "It's uh hot enough that I—actually, just take it, here. It's candy." She was rummaging through her bag as she stammered, finally feeling the tiny, hard round thing in her bag. She handed it to Qianfan and ran off to meet the others.

DEHISCENT

She didn't look back until she'd gone halfway, and she saw Qianfan sniffing the candy as he unwrapped it, held to it his lips and licked it, took a bite and grimaced as it cracked. His eyes lit up and he stared, a child bewildered and scared. She ran to Ruzhang and Wei and the Liu siblings, pretended like nothing happened. But Qianfan licked whatever sugar was still on the paper, and then wandered over, slowly, slack-jawed.

"Baba says he doesn't know how long it'll last," Zijie was saying. "So he wants us to enjoy it while we can."

"Lots of other things are broken and I think Baba can get them fixed!" exclaimed Ziqi.

"Baba doesn't *fix* anything, he calls people in to do it—stop being so silly."

Yi tuned them out. She was already sweating through her clothes and she was watching Qianfan approach, suddenly hesitant in his movement. He waited a little outside of the group and she wandered over, and once she got close enough he said, "I'm not gonna die, am I?"

Yi shook her head. "I ate a bunch earlier," she replied. "But um, please don't tell anyone else."

"What is it?"

"Candy."

"Candy?"

"Sweet . . . fruit." She shrugged. "D-Don't worry about it. I just thought you'd like it."

Qianfan nodded and nothing else.

Xie Laoshi gathered the kids—eager, for once, to sit in a room and talk about arithmetic and geometry because it meant they got a reprieve from the sauna that was outside—and Yi glanced at Qianfan, then to the others, and finally felt a little less alone. Maybe it was selfish of her to bring him into her secrets. Maybe it was worth sharing something she'd never been able to share before, that he'd never get the chance to experience otherwise.

Ruzhang's voice made her jump. "So you'll be coming more often?" he asked her.

"Yeah," Yi muttered in reply. She wondered how precarious this friendship would become. How long would it be before the questions grew more personal, before they asked about her parents and why they were never around when the rations came. Why they'd never be allowed to visit. Qianfan might ask, now. She tried not to think about that, either. "It's just . . . it's far, when it's really hot out. Worth it, though." She threw on a grin, but it felt hollow.

The day came when the house was finally done with a body. The attic door swung open, then closed, when Yi's dad went to check on it. She'd noticed he'd been doing that more now, no longer feeling the need to keep it forbidden from his daughter. The act was more disquieting than it was a relief. He decided to leave it open when he went to fetch Yi.

She followed her dad upstairs, who had a step stool in his hands, old, wooden and a dip in the middle from use.

Not much had changed. The corpses had whittled away as the house used more and more of them, exposing more muscle and bone. She was fortunate that their innards were already gone by the time the house took their muscles. A minor relief in light of things.

It was a sunny day, sunlight bright and beaming, and Yi couldn't decide whether she was comforted by the sun. It was hard to make a room of hanging corpses feel cozy and it was warm no matter the weather outside, but she was grateful for the moderate temperatures and a sky that, for the first time in a long while, was blue.

At the far end of the room hung an empty rope. It didn't matter that Yi knew where the body went; seeing the rope there, swaying slightly against the backdrop of ocean and sky, felt like a violation. Like the house was never supposed to be this way. Like the Zhu house was telling her it needed more. And here she was, helping her family prepare it.

DEHISCENT

They waited at the entrance, her dad giving her whatever time she needed. Yi stood next to him with a quiet resignation. Did it ever get easier? How had the others taken it? She turned to her father. "Hey, Baba—"

"Yes, Yi? You know, Ayeh usually helps me with this. He had to teach us."

"Us?"

Her father glanced at her hesitantly, like he'd said too much. Betrayed a thought, or a memory. He set down the stool and began to remove the rope from the rafters. "Sure, you and me."

Yi felt her suspicion creeping back around the edges. "Are you an only child too?"

He dropped the rope, holding onto the rafters with one hand and the next body's ankles with the other. "It doesn't matter," he said finally. "I'll inherit the house, as will you when you're older."

"Was Ayeh an only child?"

A beat of silence. "He had a sister. She didn't like doing this, couldn't bear to live like this. She couldn't . . . see how good we had it here." He slid over the body, then stepped down and adjusted the stool beneath the next corpse.

"Where did she go?"

"Nowhere," he said, shuffling corpses along the rafters. "Come here, Yi. Give me a hand."

"W-What if . . . I refused, Baba." Her voice shook as she even contemplated her words. How big was her family, really? How much have they kept secret from her? "I-I'm not saying I will." I don't know yet. I don't know.

"It doesn't matter," her dad repeated, a sympathetic smile on his face. He stepped down, sat on the stool, eyes level with hers. Yi kept looking at the dead eyes next to him. She couldn't help but feel, deep in her gut, that he wasn't talking about his aunt. "The house will do its job so long as it gets the care it needs."

That nagging feeling returned, an emptiness and hunger

deep in her belly, resting right up against her spine. "It's getting worse, isn't it?"

Her dad nodded. "It's bad out there."

The house seemed to breathe. Maybe it was because she knew now, had seen its beating heart. But plants popped up in the floorboards, various kinds of choy whose leaves opened and swayed as though a breeze gently swept through the house. There was fruit when she wanted it, along with the vegetables and poultry for the family's meals. Even the ginkgo branches were more fruitful than usual, which, frankly, Yi could've done without.

It took Yi a few days to realize that she had seen this happen before. It was less that the house was celebrating, even if it felt like it—after all, what reasons did it have?—and more that this seemed to happen whenever the patches of growth moved locations within the house. She stood in the hallway and frowned at the lines of yu choy that stuck up from the floor; it was going to be annoying having this growing here.

She knelt down, picked a few, and headed upstairs.

The stairs to the attic hadn't changed for her. They were still cold and forbidden, and they probably always would be. She couldn't imagine they would ever start to feel normal. Just like how her family would never really feel normal. Did they all feel like this when they learned? A twisting uncertainty of how she could possibly live in this house? How long did it take for them to accept it? She wanted to say she would run, but where would she go? She wouldn't even survive living in Fengxian like everyone else; the guilt of abandoning her family would be strong enough, but there were comforts she was too used to, as uneasy as those comforts were.

Yi went in and the sunlight welcomed her, bright and full of cheer. Her eyes fell to the corpse closest to the door and it stared back. The muscles of its head were exposed, with clouded, empty eyes and teeth bared in a permanent grin without any lips to conceal them. She didn't know why she kept coming up here—this room made her stomach lurch, made her heart leap into her throat—but here she was. If it was never going to feel normal, she should at least try to get used to the idea.

All eyes were on her.

It didn't matter if they were already dead, if anything that made it worse. It felt like the house was watching her through them, learning from her, waiting for her to make a decision.

"You first," she muttered. There was nothing *she* could do, but the house—the house could do something.

And it did.

A tin rolled out from the floorboards, the sound of something light and dry rolling around inside. It made bright, metallic *pings* as it rolled over the small imperfections of the wood. She picked it up before it hit her feet and took a look inside. It was filled with hundreds of tiny leaves, dark and shriveled, and the moment Yi opened it she knew what it was: tea. The exact kind, she was less sure.

Yi passed a few burgeoning sprouts along the main staircase. They were too young to tell what plants they were just yet, but they were already fragrant and she figured at least *this* stairwell would feel nice and welcoming soon. She couldn't help but run her fingers along the delicate sprouts, which reached toward whatever sunlight they could glean from the windows of the house. There were *some* that she could identify, like the bamboo shoots pushing their way through the walls of the foyer. She plucked one out, snapping it clean off from the base and leaving nothing but untouched wood behind. That was a spot she'd need to worry about. It was clearly going to be visible to her Baba and Ayeh's colleagues on the few occasions they dropped by, but mostly Yi worried about its size when it matured, blocking their access to the door. She pouted a little as she placed the tin of tea with the others on their dedicated shelf; she wasn't a huge fan of bamboo shoots but she was lucky enough that she could even say that.

Ayeh caught her as she left the tea room. He held out his hands and said, "Here, here . . . Let me take those." She let him. "You know, my parents used to keep a garden outside."

"What? Really?" Yi glanced at the front door, trying to imagine patches of green anywhere on the desolate earth around the house.

Ayeh nodded, a grin on his face. "Just outside. They used to grow these in normal places, like in a patch of dirt. They used to make me go outside and pick the choy for the day."

"How? Why did they stop?"

Here, her grandfather shrugged. "It was pointless," he said. "Why bother when you still had to tame it in here?"

Yi looked back at the hallway full of yu choy and nodded. She thought of her grandmother, tending to the flowers and fruit trees that didn't need to be taken care of but that she looked after anyway. Maybe they needed more maintenance than Yi thought they did after all.

For the first time in over a week, Yi felt comfortable being around her family again. She didn't talk much during dinner—it was mostly a conversation about the supply of scrap fabric and where they should be sending garments to next—but dinner finally felt normal. Or at least, as normal as it could get until she thought too hard about the house. And even then, the urge to claw through her face had faded to a distant cloud of grey dread.

"Why did you start doing this, anyway?" Yi asked. It was a question she never asked before. "The clothes, I mean."

"Everyone needs to help out," said her mother. "You do what you can."

"So . . . if I wanted to bring my friends some food or something—" Her ears burned remembering Qianfan's reaction to the hawthorn candy. She couldn't let anyone else know. She hoped he understood that too. She kind of wish he didn't. It'd free her, in a way.

"No, Yi," replied her dad.

"But why—"

"You know why."

Yi stared at her bowl of rice, pouting a little. "Okay but—" She sighed. "Okay, fine."

"I know," her mother said, sympathetically.

"Amuy has a big heart," said her grandmother. She smiled at Yi and filled her soup bowl with more broth; savoury and fragrant and filled with love. "We'll teach you to use the sewing machine. That way you can help."

After dinner, Yi pulled her grandfather into the tea room and opened the new tin. She held it up to him, hoping he could see inside. "Do you know what kind this is?" she asked. "It kind of just appeared."

Ayeh took the tin and squinted into it. He frowned. "Oolong?" he suggested. Then he smiled, an idea forming. "Why don't we brew some?" he said.

It was indeed an oolong tea. Yi recognized the smell once the leaves soaked up the hot water long enough. They sat around the tea room table and Ayeh went through the steps on how to brew it. Properly. It was a series of steps involving rinsing the tea leaves in hot water, rinsing the cups to keep them warm, pouring out the first brew to bring out the true flavours of the leaves.

"I've never done this before," muttered Yi. "It looks like too much work."

"It is," said Ayeh with a smile. "But it's a tradition. I learned it from my own grandparents."

"Here?"

He nodded. "This very room."

"I don't know if I'm going to do this again, Ayeh," she replied. "I mean, you're pouring out the first pot—I don't want to waste water!"

"Except you don't need to worry about that, do you?"

"I guess not." Yi frowned a little. Scarcity was everywhere except the Zhu house. and she wondered how long it could possibly last? Outside was dead, or at least, it was barely alive. Perhaps it was waiting, still, for a resurgence, something resilient to restore the delicate equilibrium. "How long have we had this house, Ayeh?"

"Long," he replied. "Many, many years and many, many generations. Before the world went dry and all the cities flooded. This house has belonged to our family since the seasons were dependable and emperors dressed in yellow sat on the throne."

Yi nodded and sipped on her tea.

"The house provides," he said. "It just needs some care and maintenance."

One day before school, Yi got an idea. She pulled on her shoes and held her unzipped backpack in her hands and listened for her family's morning mahjong game. The table was being set up, the clack of tiles loud and cacophonous as they spilled out onto the table. She waited for the chatter to start back up, when she was sure her parents and grandparents were ready to start their game. And when the stacking began, Yi reached over to one of the bamboo shoots jutting out of the foyer wall, stuffed it into her bag, and left the house.

She closed the door behind her firmly but quietly and waited a moment to be sure they weren't watching her. Then, she found a patch of clear ground and dug a small indent with her foot in the dry, dusty earth. It had been a particularly blustery night and the grasses around their home flash froze as they bent to the will of the wind. She fell to her knees, cracking the grass, and grabbed a nearby rock and dug in deeper. Then, she pulled out the bamboo shoot, burying the base in the ground. She wasn't sure what to expect. It sat in the dirt, tip poking up to the sky, just steps away from the stairs leading up to their porch.

A moment passed and the ground darkened around it.

Yi reached out to feel the soil, pulling away when she felt that it was wet. She watched the shoot slowly turn green, before glancing up at the attic. She could picture the bodies hanging there, the silent heart of the Zhu house working away in secret. Her heart was beating fast with anticipation and excitement, her mouth dry with nervous energy, her mind filled with flashes of images of the Zhu house surrounded by greenery, the plant life living inside of it now outside in full light of day.

She jumped to her feet, pulled on her backpack, and rushed off down the path to school.

ACKNOWLEDGEMENTS

This novella was written during a transitionary period in my writing craft, where the growing pains I was experiencing with my prose had become absolutely impossible to ignore. I struggled with this novella but finished it. Set it aside for a while and didn't even want to look at it. But Alex and Matt were ready to take on this novella for Tenebrous Press' catalogue and that was enough to propel me into a prose revision out of which emerged a novella that I'm finally happy with. So I'd like to thank them both first for believing in *Dehiscent*.

The writing of this novella could not have happened without Jade Caldwell, Colleen Mohabeer, and the people of my various Discord servers and Slacks who provided much needed accountability and/or emotional support. To Neon Yang and S.L. Huang, for their willingness to help me and for our conversations about Chinese topolects in the future. To Amal El-Mohtar, who received many a beleaguered paragraph during my prose crisis and offered me invaluable encouragement. To everyone who read my first draft while I was lamenting its state, including Meagan Hotz and Jasmine Lee. And finally, a thank you to Caleb Spassov, who reads all my first drafts except for this one—well, now you've read it, eh?

ABOUT THE CONTRIBUTORS

Ashley Deng is a Canadian-born Chinese-Jamaican writer with a love of fantasy and all things Gothic. She studied biochemistry with a particular interest in making accessible the often-cryptic world of science and medicine. When not writing, she spends her spare time overthinking society, culture and genre fiction. Her work has appeared at *Nightmare, Fireside, Augur* and others. You can find her at aedeng.wordpress.com or on Twitter at @ashesandmochi.

IVY TEAS is an illustrator & hobbyist cat spotter living beneath a clover marsh in Vancouver, Canada. She likes to make drawings conveying a sense of peering through a keyhole to observe the world—only to find that, sometimes, the world is looking right back.

TENEBROUS PRESS

aims to drag the malleable Horror genre into newer, Weirder territory with stories that are incisive, provocative, intelligent and terrifying; delivered by voices diverse and unsung.

FIND OUT MORE:
www.tenebrouspress.com
Twitter: @TenebrousPress

NEW WEIRD HORROR

CPSIA information can be obtained
at www.ICGtesting.com
Printed in the USA
JSHW021311120723
44480JS00002B/16